BY THE SEA

A tale of Liamec

J. Steven Lamperti

Copyright © 2020 J. Steven Lamperti

All rights reserved

The characters and events portrayed in this book are fictitious. Any similarity to real persons, living or dead, is coincidental and not intended by the author.

No part of this book may be reproduced, or stored in a retrieval system, or transmitted in any form or by any means, electronic, mechanical, photocopying, recording, or otherwise, without express written permission of the publisher.

ISBN-13: 978-1-7345974-2-4

Lamprey Publishing
LampreyPublishing@gmail.com

Cover design by: OliviaProDesign

Printed in the United States of America

*For Horst and Doris,
the best in-laws
anyone could wish for*

PROLOGUE

Annabelle swung the tiller to starboard as she brought the vinscif about in the wind. She kept her head down as the boom whipped across the deck. She resisted the urge to call out "hard to lee," as there was no one but her on her small sailing boat.

The wind filled the sail, and the boat heeled until the blue-gray seawater lapped at the gunwale. The sail ruffed a little, and Annabelle tightened the main sheet to make up the slack.

Annabelle felt the joy of sailing fill her. There was nothing she liked better than feeling the sea breeze in her hair and smelling the salt spray as it splashed over her clothes.

The storm winds that filled the sky and Annabelle's sail had kept some boats from the fishing fleet docked today. Annabelle had the bay to herself until the rest of the fleet returned from the deeper waters out in the open ocean.

The bay was the heart of her little town. The rough rock cliffs that lined both sides of the outlet to the ocean were the same gray stone that hung over the simple houses her fellow townsfolk all occupied.

The sky was gray, just a little less blue than the water, but the two almost matched, making the horizon sometimes hard to see. The wind whipped through the opening from the harbor out to the open ocean.

The vinscif were the small sailing boats that the people of her town had been sailing since before time began. The larger fishing ships were usually crewed by two or three men. When you traveled alone or rode the winds for pleasure, you would take a small, light vinscif.

Annabelle laughed as her boat took up speed. A distant flash of lightning brightened the dark gray clouds, and the reflected light lit up her blue-green eyes for a moment.

She turned to look at the harbor entrance and saw one of the boats from the fishing fleet tacking past the gray cliffs. It was early, but probably the storm had caused someone to call it a day.

She looked again and recognized the boat. It was her father's. She was surprised to find him being the one to head home early.

She brought her vinscif about and sailed in toward the dock. She would have to give her father grief for this. She had tried to get him to take her instead of Corentin. Her brother didn't like stormy weather, and she would have been glad to take his place.

As Annabelle jumped off the vinscif, the dock line in hand, she looked over at where her father was tying up the larger fishing vessel. It could be operated by two men, though most of the fishermen in town crewed boats of that size with three.

She felt a flash of panic. Why was her father tying up the boat himself? Usually, he'd stay at the tiller while his crew mate jumped onto the dock with the painter.

She cleated the line and ran across the boards.

"Where's Corentin?"

Her father turned to her, and she could see the streaks across his face where the sea spray had mixed with tears.

1

There was a little town called Chelle by the Sea. Chelle by the Sea was by the sea, for the sea, of the sea, and with the sea. It was practically in the sea, though it wasn't, not really. The town was, of course, a fishing town. There were people in town who did other things. Some of them, surprisingly enough, even did things that didn't have much to do with the sea. There was a cobbler; there was a schoolteacher; there was a farrier. The town didn't have a mayor, as the duke, who ruled this province in the land of Liamec, lived in his castle on a hill not very far away from town. Most of the other towns and villages in this province had a local government—all, of course, beholden to the duke. But Chelle by the Sea, due to its proximity to the ducal castle, appealed to the duke himself, or his representatives, to solve local problems.

The duke's castle was built on the hill at the top of the cliffs between Chelle and the land. The little town and its harbor were protected, sheltered, and kept apart from the mainland by rising cliffs and highlands. The primary way to Chelle, the Duke's Way, was a winding track that led from the town, up the cliffs to the lands around the duke's castle.

Around the hill that was crowned by the duke's castle was nestled the town of Ardstead. Ardstead was known, the kingdom over, for the quality of its fish exports and the exotic seafood dishes and delicacies you could get there. What wasn't as widely known was that the fish and other sea creatures that made up these recipes and exports came up the Duke's Way each morning from Chelle below.

There were small ways into town from both the east and west that wound precariously below the crags. Every few years a storm would blow in from the sea to the north, and damage one of these ways enough to make them impassable. It would take months, sometimes longer, before the trails would be repaired.

So, Chelle by the Sea was screened from the mainland by the duke and his castle. Whether it was protected, sheltered, barred, or isolated from the land depended on who you asked.

There were people in Chelle who did things other than fish, but the kings of Chelle were the fishermen. They were the kings, the princes, the earls, and even Chelle by the Sea's jesters. They ruled the town, under the auspices of the duke. There was a town council, the closest thing Chelle had to a government, composed of the most respected fishermen in town.

Now, you may ask, where were the fisherwomen? Where were the women of Chelle while the men were out fishing? Where were the daughters, mothers, and wives of these fish-gut-covered princes of the sea?

There had been, and would be, fisherwomen in Chelle. Every so often, a woman would be born, the sea in her eyes, who couldn't be dissuaded from the sea. Occasionally, one of these women would break her way through the barriers and make it into the fisherfolk's ranks. Still, most of the time, the sons would be taken out on the fishing boats, and the daughters would stay home with their mothers.

Some women fought their way out of these confines. Sometimes by finding someone to mentor them within the ranks of the fishermen of the town, and sometimes just by leaving. The pirate "Bloody Peg," who sailed the warm waters of the seas south and west of Liamec, was rumored to have been born Margaret Atwater in the little town of Chelle by the Sea.

Now, as to men or boys who might have been born without the sea in their blood, as to youths who might have enjoyed traveling by land to far-off countries, exploring, or just living in the town without venturing out on a boat each day, there actually weren't any of those ... if you asked the men on the town council.

2

There was a young woman who lived in Chelle by the Sea. Her name was Annabelle. Annabelle was neither from the sea, with the sea, nor for the sea; though of necessity, she was by the sea. She rejected the idea that she might be of the sea, though you might have thought otherwise if you gazed into her stormy blue-green eyes. The fisherfolk of Chelle were known for those eyes.

Annabelle was a little taller than most of the other young women in Chelle. She was also a little more athletic. When she was younger, she spent countless hours climbing the crags that bordered the town and swimming and splashing in the sea below those crags with her brother. Those days on the rough beaches and rocky slopes were her childhood.

She had grown, though she didn't know it, into a beauty. The swimming and climbing had wrestled strength into her young body. Her hair was the midnight black of the sea-urchins that covered the rocks of the beaches below the crags at low tide. And her eyes. Those blue-green eyes. Anyone looking into them would have been hard-pressed not to find them of the sea and would have been further hard-pressed not to drown in them.

Annabelle and her sister Bellarose lived with their parents in a little house near Chelle's western side. House is rather a generous word. The term cottage might be more applicable. As with most dwelling places in Chelle, their home was built of, and practically part of, the stone from the crags that separated and protected Chelle.

The cottage almost seemed formed from the rocks that came down from above. It was just on the seaward side of the Way that led from Chelle to the west. One reached the cottage by walking down a steep stone path to a small courtyard. Annabelle's family home was the only dwelling off this small courtyard. Above their home was the Way. Below was a steep rocky staircase that led to a small harbor. Theirs was the last home on the west side of town. Beyond the steps leading to their cottage, the narrow path wound up into the crags and finally through them to leave the sea.

Annabelle's family were the Fishers. In Chelle by the Sea, the name Fisher meant a great deal. There had been a man named Fisher on the council for at least two hundred years. Annabelle's father was fond of saying Fisher men were always fishermen, and would always be fishermen, though there were rumors he had a cousin somewhere landward who was a carpenter.

The reason for the fame of the Fisher name in Chelle wasn't just their continuing presence in town and on the town council. There were many famous men in the Fisher line. (And perhaps some women. Bloody Peg's mother's maiden name was Fisher.)

Caspian Fisher, Annabelle's great grandfather, was the source of many of the stories parents told their children on cold, windy nights in Chelle. One story was how he had rescued some fellow fishermen during what was still known as "The Great Storm." The storm had swept in so suddenly that it had caught many of the town fishers by surprise. Caspian had skillfully sailed his little vinscif around the nearby waters, warning and helping the rest of the fishing fleet make it back to safe harbor.

There was a barnacle-covered piece of dried wood hanging over the mantelpiece of their cozy little stone home. It was supposedly a piece of Caspian's vinscif. Annabelle sometimes thought it was just a shriveled-up piece of old wood that didn't look any different from the driftwood she occasionally picked up on the beach. It was one of Annabelle and Bellarose's father's chief sources of pride.

    One of the many stories told about Caspian was that he had once caught a magical fish that could talk. It offered him a wish if he threw it back into the water. Caspian threw the fish back and wished that, with his next cast, he would catch two fish. This story was told by the fishermen of Chelle as an example of how pure a fisherman Caspian was. Annabelle often hoped this one wasn't true, as she didn't want to be related to anyone so stupid.

3

Bellarose and Annabelle were hanging wash on the clothesline that stretched across the stone courtyard in front of their house. Each end of the line was clipped onto an old iron hook embedded in the stone. Annabelle sometimes thought about how long those hooks had been there, about how many generations of women named Fisher had clipped lines onto those same hooks. The salt air from the sea had corroded the iron, but it had been thick initially. Those hooks would be there and still be able to support a clothesline a hundred years from now.

The wind from off the sea was bright and lively today. The clothes would dry quickly, though they never seemed to dry completely. A slight trace of dampness and a smell lingering in the cloth always left a little vestige of the sea in them. Some days there was more sea smell to the dried clothes, some days less.

"Gunnora Poole says Danu has a torch for Delmar," said Bellarose. She turned her bright blue eyes to Annabelle to see if she was listening. Sometimes Bellarose thought Annabelle didn't really understand how important some things were. Bellarose clipped a pin onto a pair of her father's undergarments. Then she attached another. The wind from off the sea was unpredictable.

Annabelle wasn't paying attention. She was holding one of her mother's smocks loosely in one hand and gazing out to sea. Sometimes she felt as if the sea was watching her. This was one of those times.

Bellarose stamped her foot. She was half a head shorter than Annabelle, but Annabelle was reluctant to cross her when she got angry. In fact, so was everyone who knew her.

"Annabelle Agatha Fisher!" she said. "You listen to me when I'm talking to you."

"Is there something out there, Bella?" said Annabelle. She gestured out to the open waters and the gray skies to the north as she spoke.

"There's nothing out there that isn't always out there," said Bellarose. She snorted. Sometimes she felt as if *she* were the older sister.

Annabelle slowly took the smock in her hand and clipped it to the line.

"The second pin, Annabelle," said Bellarose, with a bit of annoyance. Bits of Bellarose's bright golden hair, which weren't bound in the long braid that ran down her back, tossed in the wind.

Bellarose's blond hair and blue eyes didn't just make her stand out from her sister. They made her stand out in the entire town. She had always gotten a lot of attention for her looks. When she was younger, she was teased for them. The other kids had called her things like straw head and lemon top. Now that she was older, she was getting different kinds of attention from the boys.

Annabelle's eyes turned back out to sea.

Bellarose was getting increasingly annoyed. "Annabelle," she said, "let's just finish hanging the laundry and go inside."

4

The next day, the sea left Chelle by the Sea. It wasn't that the sea itself was gone. It was still there, gray and moody as always. But the fishermen of Chelle had always felt a special connection with the sea. When they sailed out to fish on a typical day, they could feel the sea with them. They could sense the sea's support for their boats; the welcome the waves provided for their keels; the gift of power and motion the sea breezes provided their sails.

Today, this day, that welcome, that support, that gift, was not being given freely. The wind that filled the sails moved the boat forward, but it did so grudgingly. The waves parted for the boat's keel, but they resisted a little before they did so. The connection the fishermen of Chelle had with the sea was taken away.

The fishing was horrible. Nets were bringing in, at best, half of what they had brought in yesterday. One fisherman, not a Fisher of course or anyone from one of the better families, but a fisherman nonetheless, had holed his boat on a submerged rock. The other fishermen didn't feel too sorry for him, as they had told him for years that he fished too close to the Widow-maker Shoal. He had to be pulled from the sea by one of his fellows. His boat was a total loss.

Annabelle and Bellarose's father returned home late in the afternoon and left again almost immediately. The town council had called a meeting, and he needed to attend. His fishing had also been less than successful.

Annabelle thought perhaps the sea had left the town the

day before. Soon after she and Bellarose had gone inside from hanging laundry, a storm had started. The wind had blown icy rain and gray sea spray against the walls and shutters of the houses of Chelle. Most of the time, when Annabelle was sitting in her family's home, and a storm was blowing in from the sea, she felt cozy and protected by the stone walls and tightly sealed wooden shutters.

With this storm, the wind, sea spray, and frigid rain seemed to find its way through the seals around the wooden shutters and through the slats. The chilly fingers of icy, salty air seemed to find her wherever she went in the cottage. Annabelle's mother tried to start a fire, but the breezes blowing down the chimney kept putting it out.

The sea leaving Chelle was a disaster for the fishermen. Annabelle could imagine what they were talking about in the council meeting.

"How long will this last?"

"What did we do wrong?"

"What can we do?"

In a more civilized town, where the municipal flag didn't have a leaping ocean salmon on a gray background, the council might have dismissed the worries. The rigors of science and logic might have led town elders to reassure the men who came in with the fishing boats that this was in their heads. But, in Chelle, they all knew this was real. They all knew the sea could leave a town, and the people could be left bereft. The problem was, Annabelle was pretty sure, they didn't know what to do about it.

Annabelle didn't care as much as she felt she should. She was concerned about her father. She was concerned for Bellarose and her mother, and how this would affect them, but in some ways, she was happy the sea had left Chelle. She had left the sea several years ago. It kept hanging around like a jilted suitor. She was glad to see the last of it.

Bellarose wasn't the only one the boys in town had noticed in the last couple of years. Annabelle was a classic Chelle beauty. The sea in her eyes and the windswept waves in her midnight hair had drawn attention from several young men. From Annabelle's perspective, the problem was she saw them in one of two ways. Either they were brave enough to approach her, in which case they were their father's sons: proud of their fishing king heritage and proud of the sea they had in their own eyes. Or they weren't, in which case, it didn't matter.

The ones who approached her, confident their relationship with the town, fishing, and the sea, would win her over, were disappointed. Annabelle's rejection of the sea included a rejection of any boy who would look at her out of those stormy blue-green eyes that proudly announced his bond with the sea.

5

The eyes filled her vision. Not the blue-gray of a storm over the sea. Not the blue-green of the boys who had been harassing her at school and at the market. Instead, a combination of brown and gray. The color you might see in the sky when a storm flashed over a clearing in a mountain valley.

Lightning flashed, hitting the trees and mountain peaks around the valley. The eyes are angry.

Annabelle pulled her attention back from the eyes. The rest of the face filled her view. It's her brother, Corentin. She can see the anger in his eyes, and on the rest of his face. The expression on his face is a mix of sadness and anger. Not an expression she can remember ever seeing on his face and certainly not directed at her.

Annabelle tried to say something. *How can he be so angry, and why is he so sad?* She can't speak, she can only stare in guilt and sadness at her brother's angry face.

Annabelle broke down weeping. Great moaning sobs racked her body. She woke to find herself in bed, in the lower bunk of the bunk bed she shared with her sister, Bellarose cradling her head.

"I didn't want to wake you," said Bellarose, when she saw Annabelle's eyes open. She stroked a bit of sweat-dampened hair from the side of Annabelle's brow.

Annabelle continued to sob for a moment, then she tried to pull herself together.

Even with the proud name Fisher, the sisters' family was not among the wealthier families in Chelle. It was a mark of shame to Bellarose that the two of them had to share a room, let alone a bunk bed. The proud name Fisher had always meant something other than conventional success. Annabelle sometimes believed the story about their ancestor Caspian and the magic fish.

Bellarose didn't mind sharing a room with her sister. In fact, if she were honest with herself, she had to admit she liked it. What she didn't like was the impression of poverty and need it would give to her neighbors and school friends if they knew Annabelle and Bellarose had to share a room and sleep in a bunk bed.

Elle, Bellarose's former best friend from school, had gotten married. She had married Malo Netminder—a choice Bellarose questioned. Even so, Elle was the same age as Bellarose, and Annabelle was a whole year older. They were old enough to leave school and get married, like Elle. The notion that they were still sleeping in bunk beds when they were old enough to get married sent a shiver through Bellarose's body when she thought of it.

Elle left school, moved into her own home with Malo, and set up house. She was now part of the wives' circle at the market. Bellarose was sometimes astonished when she thought about the fact that someone her age, who was one of her school friends, was now part of the wives' circle at the market.

Bellarose had climbed down from the top bunk when she heard Annabelle sobbing. She was sitting next to Annabelle's pillow. Annabelle lifted her head off her sister's lap and sat up on the bunk next to Bellarose.

"Was it the same dream?" asked Bellarose.

"Yes," replied Annabelle. "He's so angry, Bella. Why is he so angry at me?"

"It wasn't your fault, Annabelle. You weren't even with them on the boat."

"That's why it was my fault," said Annabelle sadly.

6

He came down the Duke's Way. The Duke's Way was wide enough for a wagon, but it twisted and turned as it made its way down the cliffs from the lands above Chelle like a serpent. Or, perhaps, like a whip writhing through the air, swung fiercely, just about to crack.

It wasn't unusual for people to come down the Duke's Way. Merchants and transporters of goods had to go up and down. Sometimes they traveled in and out of Chelle by the east and west ways, but the Duke's Way was broader, and the windswept cliff path length was more direct. The officials from Ardstead, who came to administer the law in Chelle, also had to travel that way. There had been several wagons coming down the trail already today in anticipation of the market.

What didn't happen often was for a handsome, obviously noble-born young man to come trotting down the Duke's way on the back of a purebred milky-white stallion. The stallion picked its way delicately along the rocky road. Each step dainty. Raising its legs high, as if it were reluctant to put its hooves on the dusty rock. There was a distinct clip-clop sound each time one of its shoes hit the stone. The sound echoed off the cliff walls on either side of the Way.

There was a part of the Duke's Way that was visible from the market square below. It was early morning, and the market was getting underway. The square was slowly filling. Some booths and tents were starting to open, but most were still preparing. Some would open later. The wives' circle was beginning to gather in their spot in the center of the square by the fountain. There wasn't anything official about the wives' circle gathering in that spot. It was just where they gathered, and where they had always gathered.

The wives' circle wasn't complete yet. Not every wife in town was there every day, of course. Some days there were more and some days less. So far this morning, there were only seven or so women there. It was clear there were going to be more. The wives' circle ran by seniority. Olivia Cuttlecutter was the senior woman there at the moment. She had the helm and hoped she would keep it. Several women could take it from her by showing up today.

The earth shook—just a little. The fishermen, their families, and other merchants who were readying for the market looked up. It was just a small tremor, just enough to shift everyone's attention. The earth sometimes shook a little in Chelle by the Sea. The townsfolk thought it had something to do with being by the sea, though no one knew for sure.

Just at the moment that the earth shook, the young man on the white horse rode to the part of the Way where the path was visible from the market square. He was a good-looking young man. Pitch-black hair blowing in the sea breeze, he was tall and proud. Just at the point where a boy is no longer a boy, but you still can't see a man when you look at him.

The young man's white horse pranced across the part of the Way that was visible from below. It seemed evident to the fisherfolk and merchants watching that he wasn't aware he was being watched. He seemed oblivious to their astonished eyes. It also seemed obvious to them that someone or something did know he was being watched. Perhaps it was the horse.

Everyone in the market square watched the equestrian display. Those who didn't see it at first followed the gaze of the ones who did. When the young man rode around the corner of the Way into a part of the path that was no longer visible, there was an inaudible sigh of relief.

An immediate chatter rose among the wives' circle.

"Who is that?" said one wife.

"He's got to be of noble blood," said another.

"We've never had such a visitor from the duke's castle," said a third.

Olivia Cuttlecutter took charge. At least for the next few minutes, until someone more senior arrived, she was the leader of this group, and someone needed to settle things down before there was a panic.

"Of course we have," she said reassuringly. "Why I remember, just a few years ago, when I was fifteen, a young noblewoman from the castle came down the Way, just to see the town."

"Olivia," came a response, "you're fifty now, and we've been talking about it ever since."

There was a small collection of children in the square. In some cities, you might have thought of these as street urchins, given the way they were dressed and how poor they appeared. In Chelle by the Sea, this was just how the younger of the city's children were when they weren't in school.

As soon as the rider passed out of view, this small crowd of children split up. Almost all of them ran down the lane that led to the place where the Duke's Way entered the town. One lone child, a young boy, by the looks of him, split from the group and ran off in the opposite direction.

7

Annabelle and Bellarose led the fish wagon and the mule to the market. Even though the catch was very light yesterday, it still had to be sold. Bellarose walked on one side of Soggy's head, and Annabelle on the other.

Soggy's full name was "Soggy Swamp Head, Poop for Brains." Annabelle and Bellarose's father had named him when the girls were younger. Annabelle sometimes thought her father must have been a little annoyed at the mule when he anointed him. Annabelle and Bellarose called him Soggy.

They were leading the mule down a narrow lane toward the market square. The lane surface was the same rock as the cliffs around Chelle and the structures in the rest of town. The mule's hooves made a clunking sound that echoed off the stone walls on both sides of the lane with each step.

Sometimes Annabelle wondered how the town was carved out of the rock of the cliffs. She had asked her teacher about it, once, a few months ago.

"That's an excellent question, Annabelle," Mr. Miller said. "Though it doesn't feel like it sometimes, with the current economy, Chelle by the Sea is an ancient town with a fascinating history. It wasn't always a simple fishing village. Some aspects of the town's structure can't have been constructed without powerful magic."

Mr. Miller was the smartest person Annabelle knew. He was the teacher for the older students. Chelle by the Sea prided itself on its school system. Unlike some towns that had one-room schoolhouses, Chelle had four different classrooms. The students were divided up by age, and each of the four teachers Chelle employed had separate rooms. Mr. Miller had told Annabelle that she should call him Leonard when they weren't in class, but she didn't think that was right. He was her teacher, after all.

A boy came running down the lane toward them. Soggy pulled to the right, sharply, to avoid him. Bellarose was on that side. Soggy's head smacked into hers. Annabelle hauled back on the lead she was holding to restrain the mule.

"Ow," Bellarose cried out. She sounded angry.

"Anna," said the boy, out of breath.

"Jonah," said Annabelle, shortly. She was waiting for Bella's reaction.

"Christ on a chamber pot!" said Bellarose. Annabelle felt a little warmth creep up under the collar of her smock. She wasn't used to such language from her sister.

"Jonah," continued Bella, "what were you thinking! You can't startle a mule like that! That hurt!"

"Sorry, Bella," said Jonah. He was a small boy, not yet entered into his growth spurt. He was probably just a few years younger than Bellarose and Annabelle, but it seemed like more because of his size.

With that, Jonah ignored Bella and turned to Annabelle. Annabelle could see the storm clouds start to form in her sister's eyes.

"Anna," he said, "there's a nobleman headed to the market."

"What?" Annabelle's reply was replete with the cleverness that Mr. Miller saw in her.

"A nobleman?" said Bellarose. The storm clouds in her eyes began to part.

"He came down the Duke's Way," said Jonah, "he's riding a white horse! I thought you might want to come to see him with me, Anna."

Annabelle handed Soggy's lead to Bellarose. "Can you finish taking the fish to market, Bella?" she said, "I'm not feeling well."

8

Bellarose and Jonah led Soggy and the wagon into the market square. The market had started into full swing, though the presence of the young nobleman, who had tied up his horse and seemed to be wandering around from booth to booth, was adding an unusual dimension to the morning.

As they pulled the mule toward the Fisher booth, Bella and Jonah scanned the market for him. They could see his white horse tied up to a hitching post near the central fountain, but they couldn't see him at first. Then they saw a crowd of townsfolk, including the group of slightly dirty children that Jonah was part of earlier, around the Netminder booth. Jonah immediately took off to join his peers. Bellarose tried to peer through the crowd as she pulled Soggy onward.

Usually, there was a small pack of young men that came running over to help Bellarose and Annabelle unload the catch. Since Corentin wasn't there to help them anymore, they were mostly glad for the help. Today, there were just two waiting by the booth for Bellarose and Soggy.

"Morning, Bella," said Ewan cheerfully, as he grabbed the lead from Bellarose, and maneuvered the wagon so that the bins on the cart were next to the ones in the wooden booth. Nolan grabbed a shovel and started shoveling the fish. The catch was very light yesterday, so there wasn't too much to move.

Bella ignored them. She was staring at the crowd around the Netminder stall. It seemed like everyone who didn't have to maintain a presence in their own booth or had other business was crowded around that stall. The usual purchasers from outside Chelle were still wandering about. Almost all of them from Ardstead. Usually, they were surrounded by townsfolk trying to get their attention and get them to the right booth. Today, however, they were mostly being left alone. Bella tried to drill her gaze through the onlooker's backs to get a peek at what was happening.

Finally, some of the crowd parted enough so she could get a look. Even from across the square, and glimpsed through a mob of people, the young man cut quite a figure. He was tall and proud, and his pitch-black hair stood out among the mostly brown heads around him. Bellarose thought she saw a streak of white running through his hair, but it was hard to tell from this distance. He seemed to be carrying on a conversation with Murray Netminder. Bellarose was surprised. Malo Netminder's father, Elle's new father-in-law, was widely considered one of the less interesting (to put it politely) people in town.

"Bella!" said Ewan. He sounded annoyed. Nolan looked at her too. She realized that he'd been speaking to her for a while.

"Sorry, Ewan," she said with a smile. She had recently found that the young men of the town would often forgive her things if she smiled at them.

"Where's Annabelle?" said Nolan. He had finished shoveling the fish into the booth bins.

"She wasn't feeling well," said Bellarose. She frowned momentarily, as she wondered what had gotten into her sister.

"What's up with him?" she continued, gesturing with her chin in the direction of the young man with the black hair.

Ewan seemed annoyed again.

"I don't know, and I don't care," he said, "we've got a market to run." He strode off angrily toward his father's booth.

"Sorry, Ewan," Bellarose called out, though she wasn't entirely sure what she was sorry for. "And thank you for helping with the fish." She turned and shone her sunniest smile on Nolan.

9

Annabelle walked along the rocky beach below the cliffs near her home. The dark gray rocks loomed overhead, while the wind and salt spray were moaning as they struggled their way through the crevices in the granite stone walls. The narrow beach was nothing but a thin ribbon of rounded pebbles that marked the delineation between the base of the cliffs and the start of the gray ocean waters.

Annabelle walked barefoot along the sea-smoothed rocks, carrying her shoes in her hand. When she got to the rocky part just a little ahead, she would have to put them back on. In some places, the rocks of the shore were worn smooth by the countless years of pounding ocean waves, but in others, there were sharp edges and rough surfaces that would cut her feet like a knife.

The shoreline Annabelle walked along was accessible from the small harbor below her house. For the most part, it couldn't be seen from the Western Way out of Chelle. Some parts could, however, especially if you were on the edge of the Way, leaned out over the cliff's brink, and gazed below.

If Annabelle looked up, she might have seen a small head covered in thick, tousled brown hair peering down at her. Jonah had left the crowd of youngsters stalking the stranger in the market square and went off in search of Annabelle. He called out. "Annabelle!" But the sound got lost along with the wind and the salt spray among the rocky crevices of the gray granite cliffs.

It was not possible to scale the cliffs. Jonah took off back toward the narrow path down from the Western Way to the courtyard where Annabelle's home was, then down to the harbor, and finally to the beach below.

He ran most of the way. By the time he reached Annabelle at the end of the pebble beach, he was out of breath.

Annabelle turned to him. Strands of her black hair drifted in the salt breeze from the sea.

"Jonah," she said calmly.

"Huh," said Jonah with a pant.

Annabelle nodded and turned her attention back to the rocks in front of her. They stood at the edge of the pebble beach. The beginning of a rock shelf that ran further along the shoreline was in front of them. Indentations in the stone were worn into steps by countless feet over the years. It formed a sort of ladder or staircase from the beach up to the top of the shelf.

It wasn't terribly high or really that steep. If Jonah hadn't been out of breath, he probably would have clambered up and offered his hand to Annabelle. If she hadn't been wearing the skirts that her mother made her wear nowadays, she would have been at the top in a flash without help. The skirts did make it more complicated, and Jonah was so out of breath that he wasn't any use.

Annabelle held the skirts up with one hand so as they wouldn't hinder her feet. She reached up with the other arm to get a grip on the top of the rock face. It felt as if the skirts were designed to make this harder, she thought with a scowl.

When they both reached the top, they sat on the rocks for a moment. Annabelle waited for Jonah to catch his breath.

"You could have let me rest at the bottom," he said with a trace of a frown.

"Why aren't you still hanging out with the other kids at the market?" said Annabelle. "I thought this nobleman on the white horse would keep you busy all day."

"I'm not a kid anymore, Anna. I'm fourteen, almost fifteen. Father's going to take me out on the fishing boat regularly next season," said Jonah. The frown deepened.

"I know you're not, Jonah," said Annabelle with a smile.

The smile was enough for Jonah, and he forgave her. For that smile, he probably would have forgiven her for even more than that.

"Why'd you leave the market?" he said.

Annabelle kicked her shoes off onto the stone of the shelf, careful to avoid kicking them into a tide pool, and stretched her toes out in the sea air. It was her turn to frown.

"I don't care about any stupid nobleman in the market. I want things to be the way they used to be."

"Before your brother?" said Jonah.

"Before," said Annabelle.

10

Annabelle was lying on the lower bunk when Bellarose burst through the door. The shutters on the little window in their bedroom were open, and a salty sea breeze was trailing across the sill into the room.

"His name is Llyr," said Bellarose breathlessly.

"Whose name?" said Annabelle, trying to sound disinterested, though she was pretty sure she knew who they were talking about.

"Whose name!" said Bellarose with a snort. Bellarose tried her best to make her snort the most derisive sound possible. However, coming through her freckled nose, it still sounded dainty.

"He is so pretty, Anna," continued Bellarose. "He looks like a god."

Annabelle rose to her side, leaning on one elbow. Despite herself, Bellarose's excitement was contagious. "Did you talk to him?"

"Did I talk to him! Annabelle, where's your head been at the last couple of days? Of course, I didn't talk to him. He just came down from the duke's castle, riding a white horse! He's a gentleman. Did I talk to him!" Bellarose shook her head in disbelief.

Annabelle just waited. She knew she wouldn't have to say much of anything to get more out of Bellarose.

"He spent a lot of time in the market. He walked around, talking to lots of people. Some of the merchants from Ardstead tried to talk to him, but he seemed to want to talk to people from Chelle more." Bellarose paused her breathless recital for a moment to look proud.

"He talked for a long time to Murray Netminder. Murray Netminder! That's how you know he was not from here because no one from around here would spend that much time talking to Murray Netminder. He stopped at the Cuttlecutter booth. He talked to the wives' circle for a bit."

Annabelle just watched her sister for a moment. She could tell that Bellarose was still somewhere in the middle of her recitation. Nothing would stop her until she was finished.

"He's so pretty, Anna," Bellarose said again. "He has black hair with a little white streak running down the front. It looks a little like a bolt of lightning, but it splits at one end. He wore a dark blue shirt. It looked so soft and moved funny. I think it might have been silk. I've never seen silk."

Bellarose paused for a moment. She considered whether her failure to identify if the shirt was silk or not jeopardized her telling of the story.

"His pants were brown—fancy, with sewn-up cuffs and everything. And, you know what, Anna? I think that his pants had pockets sewn into them. Instead of having a pocket tied to his belt, I think there's one inside his pants. I saw him reach in and pull out a coin to throw it to one of the kids in the market.

"And Anna," here Bellarose paused again, and Annabelle saw her eyes start to tear up a little, "the horse." Bellarose choked a bit when she tried to speak. She stopped, cleared her throat, and started again. "The horse is the most divine thing I've ever seen. He's huge. Bigger than any horse ever. He looks so smart. He was tied up by the fountain the whole time Llyr was in the marketplace, but he didn't seem impatient. He just watched everything going on around him. A couple of times, I thought he noticed me. He's the color of the top of a wave cresting. You know, the bit of white foam at the very top of a wave as it's breaking out in the open ocean? He's that exact color."

Bellarose paused for a breath. She looked as if she needed it.

"After he spoke to Murray, he talked to some of the other fishermen. Afterward, I asked, and they said he was asking them about their catches and about fishing. They said he seemed very knowledgeable. Can you believe that Anna, a nobleman who is interested in fishing?

"Anna, he's staying at the Sea Chelle Inn! He's staying in town! I talked to Olive. She told me her father fixed up his best room. She said when her father found out that he wanted to stay there, he practically shat himself. He spent the whole afternoon trying to get the room good enough."

Annabelle looked at Bellarose. She knew her sister well enough to know that the climax was coming.

"That's not the end of it, Anna," she continued, "Murray told me that he asked about the town, and about the families in town. About the best and oldest families. He knew something about Caspian Fisher. He asked about the Fisher family! He even asked where we live! He asked about us!"

11

That day, the sea was still gone from Chelle. While their wives, daughters, young sons, and aged fathers sold the fish and other sea creatures they caught the day before, the fishermen of Chelle were again rejected by their lifelong lover, master, and servant, the sea.

The winds blew unfavorably no matter which direction you wanted to go. The waves would sweep across the gunwale, flooding the deck, regardless of which way the boat was headed. The nets would come back empty, or mostly empty, even in the particular spot where your family had fished for generations.

After unloading their meager catches, the town council had met for the second straight day. This was quite unusual. The town council commonly met once a month.

There was talk, in the council meeting, of sacrificing a bull to Poseidon. This was old-fashioned talk and was considered unscientific by some of the council members. It was thought to be blasphemous by others. A quiet battle had been going on in Chelle for a long time. Things moved slowly in Chelle, and while the "new" religion of Christianity was strong in town, the old gods still lingered.

There was a church in town and a priest. He wasn't, however, on the council, as he wouldn't know a haaf-net from a salmon putcher. Many of the council members would make an appearance at his church on Sunday; however, some of those were strong supporters of the bull sacrifice idea being floated at the meeting.

Even the members that were proud and happy to attend

church service each Sunday morning had conflicted feelings about this question. Poseidon was the god of the sea and the waves. While Jesus was supposed to be the god of everything, sometimes you needed to call in a specialist. If you asked Poseidon what a haaf-net was, it seemed clear that he would have a correct answer.

Also, you couldn't sacrifice a bull to Jesus. They mostly knew that, even without asking the priest. You couldn't sacrifice a bull to Jesus, and they really felt the need to do something.

In the end, the council stopped short of authorizing the bull sacrifice. Several members were disappointed, but the nays outweighed the ayes. Someone was dispatched to the priest requesting that he have the congregation pray for the town and the sea's return. Many of the members went home after the meeting and performed their own personal appeals to Poseidon.

12

Annabelle was the last one to get up the next morning, so she was still in bed when the morning's preparations were interrupted by a knock on the door. It was early enough that the only people up were fishermen getting ready for the day or fisherfolk getting the previous day's catch to market.

Bellarose was in the main room. She jumped when she heard the knock at the door. It wasn't a loud knock. It was quiet, almost polite. It was, however, insistent. It was the kind of knock that wasn't going to let itself be ignored.

Bellarose squealed. Not an animal-like squeal. More lady-like. The sort of squeal that a dignified lady who had only her family's best interests at heart might give out in a moment of uncertainty or distress. At least that's what Bellarose told herself.

People did occasionally knock on the door. Just not this early in the morning. Bellarose crossed over to the door of her parent's room, where her father was getting ready for his fishing day.

"Papa, there's someone at the door," She hissed urgently.

"Well, see who it is, Bella," her father said calmly.

Bellarose crossed back over to the door. There wasn't a window near the doorway, so there was no way to see who was outside. She opened the door and peeked out.

It was a kind of worst-case scenario for Bellarose. With him asking about the Fisher family and where they lived yesterday, and the early morning knock, the possibility that it might be the young nobleman had crossed her mind and terrified her.

It was him. "Llyr," her frenzied brain tried to tell her. He was just as good-looking as he had seemed yesterday in the market, but now, here he stood just a few feet in front of her. Seeing him up close like this, a couple of things she hadn't seen from a distance the day before forced themselves on her attention.

The white streak in his black hair cut diagonally across his forehead until it ended in three locks of snow-white hair that hung just above his eyes. Those eyes were eerily familiar to Bellarose. They were the blue-green sea eyes that she saw every day among her classmates and fellow residents of Chelle. Somehow this nobleman who had come riding down the Duke's way from Ardstead had stolen his eyes from the fisherfolk.

Llyr held his horse's lead loosely in his hand. The horse stood just behind him, with his head over one of Llyr's shoulders. His head was turned slightly, and one large blue eye was gazing soulfully into Bellarose's.

Llyr raised one hand, the one without the lead in it, and started to speak.

Bellarose slammed the door. She darted back over to her father's room.

"Papa," she blurted out, "it's that nobleman, the one I told you about from the market. He's here!" Her words got higher and higher pitched as she spoke. If a dog had been present, his or her ears might have been injured by the last word's pitch.

Bellarose's father looked confused.

"Here?" he repeated. He shook his head in disbelief, then he looked a little annoyed. "I'm getting ready to go out on the boat for the day. What could someone like him want with us?"

"What should I do, Papa?" said Bellarose.

"Well, I suppose we better see what he wants."

13

Annabelle woke with a start. She had been having such a sweet dream. Corentin, who was often in her dreams these days, was happy for once. They were climbing on the crags between the beach and the Westward Way, as they used to. Corentin usually led, and she followed, not because he was a boy, and she was a girl, but because he was a year older and she looked up to him.

Just before she woke, he was reaching down from a ledge above her. His outstretched hand looked so familiar to Annabelle. The tanned skin, the scraped knuckles. She reached up to grasp his hand, felt the warmth of her brother's strength as he started to help her climb up to the ledge, and then woke to Bellarose jumping onto her bunk.

"Anna," shrieked Bellarose, "he's here! He's here!"

"Who's here, Bella?" Annabelle asked, after a brief pause to replace the windy rock face in her awareness with her bedroom.

"Llyr," said Bellarose. She stopped for a second realizing that she had just said his name as if she knew him personally. She had a moment of doubt about how appropriate that was, just a moment.

"He's outside, talking to Papa!" she continued. "I opened the door for him! Papa didn't let him in! He's talking to him outside on the stoop!"

"Quietly, Bella," said Annabelle. "You're going to wake Poseidon's brother."

Poseidon's brother was, of course, Hades. It wasn't usually considered a good idea to wake the lord of the underworld.

This was a common expression in Chelle. Before the arrival of Christianity, a mere thousand years, or so, ago, beliefs in Chelle by the Sea were very focused on the worship of Poseidon.

Bellarose continued, a little more quietly, if not more calmly.

"I opened the door for him. I guess I opened the door for him twice. I asked him. I said, 'What can we do for you?' Guess what, Anna? He knew my name! He said, 'You must be Bellarose.' He knew my name!"

"That's great, Bella," said Annabelle. She got up and started to get dressed. "How soon is he going to go away, and what does he want?"

"He's talking to Papa. I don't know what he wants. He told me he wanted to talk to Papa."

"Bella," said Annabelle calmly as she laid her hand on her sister's shoulder. "If he told you he wanted to talk to Papa, then you know what he wants."

Bellarose looked at Annabelle with obvious disgust. "I don't know what he wants to talk to Papa about," she said firmly.

Annabelle finished getting dressed.

"Annabelle," came their father's voice calling from the other room, "could you come here for a moment, please."

14

Annabelle's father stood on the stone of the courtyard in front of the cottage. As Annabelle went out through the door into the briny gray morning air, he turned to her. "Annabelle," he said, "this gentleman," and here he made an openhanded gesture toward Llyr, "has asked my permission to walk and talk with you."

Llyr was near the edge of the courtyard. The gray sea sky was behind him, and the light filtering through the clouds silhouetted him. Annabelle lost her breath for a second when she looked at him. He was everything that Bellarose had said, and perhaps a little more.

He wore the dark blue silk shirt that Bellarose had mentioned, and as the morning breeze shifted the fabric, she could make out the outline of his chest. He was tall, towering over her father. His hair was black as midnight, and the bolt of white that split his forelock almost glowed in the gloom of the overcast morning.

For a moment, Annabelle was stricken and found herself drawn to this beautiful young man. Then, she looked into his eyes. The sea was gazing at her out of those eyes. The same blue-green that she wore. It was almost like looking into a mirror. Annabelle grew angry. Her memories of her brother came flooding into her. For a moment, she wanted to slap the smug, satisfied smile off the perfect, pretty face looking down at her.

Her father was talking. Annabelle realized that he had been talking for a little while now. She focused her attention on what he was saying.

"... modern world. Don't you agree, Annabelle?"

"Of course, Father," she said. She didn't want to contradict him in front of this young man, whose presence she suddenly found insufferable.

"I'm glad you agree," said her father. He moved back to the door to the cottage, opened the door, went inside, and closed the door behind him.

Annabelle felt betrayed and a little lost. What was she supposed to do now?

Llyr looked at Annabelle for a moment. Then he stepped forward and said, "I suppose introductions are in order. I'm Llyr, and this is Breaker." He pulled gently on the lead, and the white horse that stood behind him moved forward. The stallion pushed its head against Annabelle. It was a friendly gesture, but even so, with the horse's size and strength, she was staggered and had to step back to regain her balance.

"I hoped," said Llyr in a silvery voice almost as beautiful as his face, "that we could take a walk along the shore."

15

Annabelle and Llyr walked along the pebble beach below the Way. The same beach that she walked with Jonah just the day before. She wished he were here instead of this intimidating stranger.

A pebble from the beach had worked its way into Annabelle's shoe and was hurting her toe. She was embarrassed to take her shoes off in front of Llyr. He was saying something, trying to give her some background about his family, but she was distracted by the pain.

"Can I take my shoes off?" she said, interrupting him. He was complaining about his brother. Something about him being bossy, Annabelle didn't have much patience. Everyone had issues with someone bossy in their family. "I usually walk barefoot along the beach."

"Of course," said Llyr. He looked a bit taken aback at being interrupted but made the transition with grace.

Llyr stepped in front of Annabelle, dropped to one knee in the sand, and reached out to her right ankle. He lifted her leg a little and gently pulled the shoe off her foot. Annabelle didn't know how to react. She wasn't used to having anyone do things for her, and seeing a nobleman on one knee in front of her was not something that she had ever conceived. Llyr repeated the action with her left ankle.

Annabelle found herself looking at his knee on the smooth damp pebbles. The brown material of his pants was fine. Finer than any fabric that she had ever seen, except perhaps for his shirt. She could see a stain starting to form on the cloth as the seawater from off the pebbles seeped into the material. She felt a moment of sadness.

Llyr rose and handed her shoes to her with a graceful bow. "Your footwear, my lady." Annabelle noticed that he didn't make any attempt to take his own shoes off. They, as all of his clothes, were fancier than anything she had ever seen. They were polished brown leather with a pointed toe. They practically shone with reflected light from the glints of sunlight that worked their way through the gray clouds and bounced off the small waves making their way up the beach.

As they continued along the shore, Annabelle asked the one question that she had been wondering about since Llyr arrived in Chelle. Certainly, since he had come to their home this morning.

"Why are you here, sir?"

Llyr looked wounded. "Annabelle, please! Call me, Llyr."

"Llyr," she corrected herself. "Why are you here, Llyr?"

16

Llyr paused for a moment. He took up a pose on the beach—a showman's pose. For a moment, he looked like one of the bad actors at the playhouse posing during a soliloquy in a Greek drama. He even had one hand lifted with his palm turned upward toward the sky.

Chelle by the Sea had a small playhouse. The actors were the fishermen and other citizens of the town, not anyone more knowledgeable in the fine art of acting. It did, however, provide entertainment for some of the citizens of Chelle. So Annabelle was quite capable of recognizing melodrama.

"Annabelle," Llyr began, "a name to shout to the stars." Llyr lifted his upraised hand higher as he spoke and burned his gaze into Annabelle's eyes. "A beauty to compare to the heavens. Hair as mysterious as midnight, a complexion that flies with the snows of winter, a face to make the angels cry, and eyes that put the sea waves to shame."

Llyr's gaze seared deeper and deeper into Annabelle's consciousness with each word. It wasn't just that he had the blue-green waters of the sea in his eyes. It was more that his blue-green eyes were the sea.

"Annabelle," Llyr continued, "fated to be the queen of the universe. Doomed to be the new Helen of Troy. Wars will be fought over you. Men will die for you. The name Annabelle Agatha Fisher is spoken far and wide as the name of the most beautiful woman in Liamec!"

Annabelle shook herself. She stepped backward on the beach's salty pebbles and said, "No, it's not."

A wave rolled up onto the beach. Annabelle was facing the sea and took a step back to avoid the water. Llyr was facing Annabelle, with his back to the ocean. The water flowed up the beach and over his pretty leather shoes. For a moment, there was a flash of anger on his face. He looked down at his feet, then at the wave, and finally at the sea. He seemed personally affronted at the insolence.

"Why are you here, Llyr?" Annabelle repeated.

17

Llyr's momentary flash of anger dissipated. He smiled at Annabelle. His smile was like the sunlight shining through the clouds as they opened after a storm swept through the harbor in Chelle. It broke the gray clouds open and bathed sunshine on everything below.

"There's no fooling you, is there?" he said.

Annabelle just waited.

"I've seen you, Annabelle," Llyr said, "watched you. This town, these people, they don't appreciate you. They don't see your love for the waters, for the sea. They don't think a woman can fish the waves as well as any man."

Annabelle felt a chill. She resisted the urge to look from side to side to see if anyone was watching them right now. She backed away a step.

"You can sail rings around any of them. If they let you, you could out fish any of them as well. I see the spirit of your ancestor Caspian Fisher in you. If they let you have a chance, you could rule this town!" Llyr got excited again. His hand was beginning to reach for the sky.

"You're barmy," said Annabelle. She turned and started to run down the beach toward the stone stair that led back up to her home. Her bare feet slipped a little on the rounded pebbles.

"Wait, Annabelle," Llyr called out urgently, "I was kidding. I've just seen you in the market square, and thought you looked nice, interesting."

Annabelle stopped and turned back to Llyr. "When were you in the market square?"

"Sorry," said Llyr. He looked a little embarrassed. "I get carried away sometimes."

"When were you in the market square?" Annabelle repeated.

Llyr smiled again. Despite herself, Annabelle couldn't help but feel the warmth and charm in his smile. He hesitated for a moment as if thinking about how to answer.

"I've been sneaking into town for a few weeks, disguised as a merchant. I've been with the convoys from Ardstead. I've been keeping a low profile. I wanted to see, and know, Chelle before visiting."

"Why would you come to visit Chelle in the first place?"

"You know, it's funny. You people live here, but you have no idea where you live. Chelle by the Sea is the oldest fishing village on the Liamec coast. There have been people fishing here for thousands of years. The stones of your houses, roads, and harbors were formed from cliffs and cut from the sea by mages from ancient times. Your town has more history and more connection with the sea than any place in the world. People were worshiping Poseidon here a thousand years before Jesus was born."

Annabelle had learned a little about the history of Chelle by the Sea from Mr. Miller. It was nothing compared with what Llyr knew. They spent half an hour walking along the beach, discussing the ancient sea worship of the town.

Sometimes Annabelle wondered why every house she ever entered in Chelle had a little alcove off the central living area. In some households, these had become Christian shrines, with statues of Jesus, crucifixes, or portraits of Mary. In many, they continued to be dedicated to the sea.

In the end, Annabelle found herself having a good time. When she and Llyr returned to the house, and he left, she was relieved, but not as relieved as she had expected to be. She was, however, happy it was over, and her life would be returning to normal.

18

Jonah was at the door. Bellarose opened it. He held a little bundle of white sea thrift flowers in his hand, the flower that was locally called Poseidon's dander. Bellarose just stood for a moment and looked at him. Then she smiled, turned toward the cottage's backrooms, and called out, "Annabelle, you have a suitor!"

"Jonah," said Annabelle calmly, when she came to the door.

"Anna," said Jonah. He looked at the floor and thrust out his hand with the flowers clenched in his fist.

"Why, thank you, Jonah," said Annabelle. She took the flowers, reached out with her other hand, and ruffled his unruly mop of brown hair.

Jonah pulled his head back when he realized what she was doing. "I wondered if you wanted to go to the church dance on Sunday," he said.

"Bellarose and I are going to be there," said Annabelle. "Now, if you'll excuse me, Jonah, I had something I wanted to talk to Bella about. Thank you for the flowers, they're lovely."

She closed the door.

"Bella," said Annabelle, a little later. "Where do you think Corentin is?"

"Anna," said her sister, "why can't you let him rest in peace? You know where he is. He's at the bottom of the ocean."

"No," said Annabelle, "I mean his spirit. Where's his spirit?"

"In Hades, where all spirits go when people die." It wasn't as dangerous or unlucky to talk about Hades the place, as it was to talk about Hades the God. Places don't have ears.

"It's not fair," said Annabelle, "he was so young and such a good person."

"I'm sure the judges of the dead sent him on to the Elysium fields. I'm sure they looked at him and found it to be an easy decision. I'm sure he's happier than we are. After all, he doesn't have to hang up his parents' undergarments."

19

The sea returned to Chelle the next day. Coincidentally, that day, Llyr left the Sea Chelle Inn and was expected to ride his white horse up the Duke's Way to Ardstead in the evening. Both of these things made Annabelle breathe a sigh of relief.

The fishermen were all relieved as well. When they put to sea that morning, the winds and waves were welcoming. They felt the warmth of a lover embracing them after a long cold absence.

However, some of the more sensitive fishermen weren't so sure about the completeness of the return. It didn't feel as if their lover was back for good. More like, she had come in the door, announced her arrival, and then started listing conditions. It felt probational. There was something they needed to do, or not do, to assure the sea stayed with the town.

Unfortunately for the fishermen of Chelle by the Sea, the sea didn't come with an instruction text. They had no idea what they needed to do to get back into the sea's good graces, permanently.

Bellarose was in the market square. She and Annabelle had already run the booth for the morning, and Annabelle had left to take Soggy and the cart home. Bellarose was taking the rare opportunity of a little free time to browse some of the merchant's booths. She loved digging through the stalls with bolts of cloth, clothes, and ribbons. She didn't have enough money to buy anything, but she enjoyed looking all the same.

She walked past the central fountain on her way to a booth on the opposite side of the square. The wives' circle came toward her. They didn't approach her as a group of people, or even as a crowd of individuals. They came from around behind the fountain, flocking like a flight of birds. The flock wheeled around the fountain's corner, then arranged themselves in front of Bellarose in a semicircle.

Mrs. Cuttlecutter was again senior at the moment; she'd been having a fortunate run of leadership. Perhaps her elders were starting to show their ages. She stepped to the fore and spoke for the group.

"Bellarose Fisher," she said.

Bellarose wasn't too happy with this development. The wives' circle was a force in Chelle, and you didn't want to get on their bad side. Though she couldn't imagine what she might have done.

"Yes?" she said hesitantly.

"What," Mrs. Cuttlecutter hesitated after this word. She found that a pause at the right moment added weight to what she said. Sometimes she felt that she paused at the wrong moment, but this time, she felt reasonably confident, "was your sister doing with that nobleman, yesterday?" Curiosity was a flame in Mrs. Cuttlecutter's gray linen-clad chest. The need to know more about what went on in Chelle was a very important part of the wives' circle's purpose for being.

"I don't know," said Bellarose. She looked from side to side. The wings of the semicircle were starting to close around her.

"Sometimes, I think," said Mrs. Cuttlecutter, "that you Fishers think you're better than the rest of us." Several of the women in the circle nodded their heads at this.

Mrs. Netminder cut in, "Did he come to town just to see Annabelle?"

The widow Poole spoke up, "How did he know who she was?"

Bellarose looked from side to side again. Desperate for a way to escape. For a moment, she thought she saw an opening. One of the wives was Elle, her friend, who had left school to get married.

Bellarose turned toward Elle and said her name. She hadn't meant it to, but her voice came out sounding rather plaintive.

"Elle!"

Elle looked startled for a moment at being singled out. She hesitated a second, then pushed the wife beside her away, opening a gap in the semicircle.

"Run, Bella," she shouted.

20

Llyr rode Breaker along a dark shadowy lane, which led to the base of the Duke's Way. The evening was overcast, and a light drizzle was in the air. It was the type of rain that made you wonder if it was really raining or if it was only a heavy fog. Llyr had pulled a thick brown cloak over his shoulders to keep off the evening chill and, perhaps, to intercept a few of the bigger drops. He rode along at a slow trot, just a bit faster than a jog. Normally he would have been walking Breaker along this street, but he hoped to get a good part of the Duke's Way under Breaker's hooves before the drizzle turned to real rain.

A small figure appeared out of the shadows in the lane in front of the horse.

Llyr made no effort to stop. Now, whether he saw the small figure and just didn't think there was any significance to it, or he didn't see the figure at all due to the shadows and lighting is not for us to judge. Breaker did, however. The horse reared back. The sound of the horse's hooves coming to a sudden stop echoed off the stone walls of the buildings on both sides of the lane.

The moon broke through the clouds for a moment, and the small figure was suddenly bathed in moonlight. Llyr settled Breaker, looked at the little boy standing in his path, and started laughing.

"Can I help you, grub?" he said.

Jonah straightened himself, shook a bit of rain off his gray linen tunic, and said, "You better leave Annabelle alone."

Llyr looked serious for a second. He leaned forward over

the pommel of his saddle and said, "And why is that?"

Jonah straightened again. Standing as tall as he could, he tried to stare directly into Llyr's eyes. It was hard, as Breaker was stepping a little from side to side, and the boy stood on the ground, looking up into the eyes of a man sitting far above him. The boy was dressed roughly. The young man had on fine clothes. The boy had tousled brown hair, slicked back by the rain. Llyr had his hair of midnight black with the forked streak of white. But, the eyes were almost a match. The waters of the sea stared out of the boy's eyes into the eyes of the man.

"I'm gonna marry her!" said Jonah with determination.

Llyr laughed again. He guffawed. He cackled. He chuckled, giggled, and snickered. He didn't howl, but almost.

"You're a shrimp, a sprout, a seedling. You're a runt, a trifling, a child. Don't you think that she's a little out of your class?"

"She's only two years older than me," Jonah said indignantly. "I'm going to be helping crew my father's fishing boat next season."

Llyr stopped laughing. He smiled down at Jonah. "Well," he said, "it's important to know the competition." He spurred Breaker to one side to walk him around Jonah.

Jonah stepped aside. This was as far as his confrontation plan went.

Llyr started riding around the boy. Suddenly he stopped and almost keeled over in the saddle. He slumped to one side and let out a moan.

Jonah jumped to the side of the horse to stop the larger man from falling.

"Are you all right?" he asked.

Llyr groaned and sat up straighter on Breaker's back. He seemed to be pulling himself together.

"It's nothing," he said, "just a little flash of precognition. Something I got from one of my relatives."

"Precognition?" said Jonah. "What's that? Is it something like the flu?"

"Something like that," said Llyr.

Jonah took a step back. He looked suspiciously at Llyr. "Is it catching?"

Llyr pressed his knees into Breaker's sides and rode on down the lane.

Jonah stood for a moment in the drizzle, watching the white horse and rider as they started the climb up the Duke's Way.

21

Bellarose rushed into the room and flopped down on Annabelle's bunk. "Tell me every detail," she said. "What did he say? What did you say? How cold was it on the beach? Everything."

"I told you all that already yesterday," said Annabelle.

"I know," sighed Bellarose, "but you didn't tell it right."

"I told it the way it happened."

"You left out all the important stuff. Did the white streak in Llyr's hair glow in the sunlight? Did he gaze longingly into your eyes? Did he try to kiss you?"

Annabelle snorted at her sister. "Why would he try to kiss me? I'm just glad it's over. Now that he's gone, we can all return to normal."

After the market the next day, Annabelle and Bellarose had school. They had school three days a week in the afternoon for two hours. Some older folk of the village didn't understand why the town wasted so much time on schooling. "There isn't that much stuff to learn," one of the older fishermen was heard to say to another, "Why I never went to school at all, and I know everything I need to know."

In fact, they used to have school only two days a week, but when they added Mr. Miller to the school staff a few years ago, he had pushed for the addition of Wodensday to the schedule. In some ways, Chelle by the Sea was a very progressive town.

After school, Annabelle stayed behind and asked Mr.

Miller about the things she and Llyr had talked about.

"Those are excellent questions, Annabelle," he said. "It sounds as if this Llyr fellow had access to some interesting books. I'll have to see if I can get a chance to talk to him some time.

"The village of Chelle does have a history of the worship of Poseidon, the god of the sea. Christianity has replaced it, to a certain degree, but it still lingers in many of the nooks and crannies of the town.

"Those alcoves you noticed in most of the houses in town were dedicated altars to Poseidon and the sea. The less respectful call them brine shrines. They would be decorated with symbols of Poseidon: horses, waves, earthquakes, and tridents.

"One of the more common features would be some kind of sacrifice to the god of the sea. A fish, some seaweed, or perhaps some seashells. This is why, to this day, when you visit in some houses in the town, you can detect a distinct fishy smell."

Annabelle enjoyed Mr. Miller, but as with most teachers in her experience, it seemed to be very easy to get them to start lecturing.

"I've noticed this phenomenon increasing recently," continued Mr. Miller. "It seems that some of our older village residents have been making sacrifices at their shrines to help with the current fishing problems. While the spirit of the sea was gone from Chelle, I've been a little careful about which families I visit, for fear of the smell."

22

As the Fisher family sat down to their repast that evening, Mrs. Fisher tried to get Annabelle and Bellarose to talk about what their teacher had said in school. There was no such attempt to get Mr. Fisher to talk about his day. For one thing, she knew what he would talk about if she did. For another, on the previous occasions when she had succeeded in getting him to talk about his day fishing, she had regretted it afterward. Surprisingly, just like the night before, fish was what was on the table.

As the family sat down, the sound of a rider on the pathway outside intruded. This wasn't the sound that the unshod mule Soggy's hooves made on the stone of the path, this was the sound of iron horseshoes as they clanged off the rocky trail.

The path from the Way down to the courtyard outside the Fisher's home was narrow and steep. Soggy was very familiar with it, but an unfamiliar horse and rider were going to find it difficult going. The clang of each individual hoof was separated by a bit of time as the horse delicately picked his way down the tricky trail. The Fishers had time to speculate about who might be visiting them.

"I'll get the door," said Bellarose. She was the only member of the Fisher family who appreciated their newfound popularity.

Mr. Fisher looked at his wife and sighed. The open ocean was his habitat. While he was ashore, he appreciated nothing more than being left alone.

She looked back at him and poked him with a long bony

finger. "Angus Fisher! You do not let your daughter answer the door to a stranger while you just sit here. What would the neighbors think? Get up right now!"

Mr. Fisher opened the door before the knock. There was a horse and rider, as the family expected, out in the courtyard. The traveler was just dismounting. Both the rider and the horse were silhouetted against the evening sky. The setting sun turned the gray sky a beautiful shade of chestnut brown fading to orange nearer the horizon. The horse was a roan stallion, his colors gray and brown. The colors of the horse seemed to match the sky, making him look almost transparent.

The rider finished his dismount and looked over at Mr. Fisher standing in the open doorway. He was a distinguished, older-looking gentleman dressed all in blue. He tied up his horse and walked over toward the door. He must have ridden through a rain shower as he rode along the Way, as his clothes were a little damp. The blue jacket he wore looked like velvet, though soggy velvet.

Bellarose hovered over Mr. Fisher's shoulder. As the stranger came to the doorway, she squeezed beside her father, so the two of them stood side by side.

"Hail, good sir," said the man. On closer inspection, his jacket looked like a messenger's livery. "I have a message to deliver to Annabelle Agatha Fisher."

Mr. Fisher nodded an acknowledgment. The messenger stepped up to Bellarose, executed a little half-bow, and reached out to grasp her hand. He lifted her hand, pressed the back of it to his lips.

Bellarose giggled. He had a bristly, stiff white-haired mustache, and it tickled the back of her hand as he kissed it.

"That's my sister," she said breathlessly. "Annabelle," she called out, a little too loudly, as Annabelle and their mother were not very far away.

Annabelle came forward. Bellarose moved a little to the side to give her access to the door. The messenger executed another half-bow toward Annabelle, this time. He was handsome in his way, but Annabelle wasn't sure about how his eyes popped out. Also, his face, especially around the lips, was a little moist as well, perhaps from the rain shower he had ridden through on his way here.

His bow was very graceful, however. He made a smooth hand gesture toward Annabelle as he bowed, and when his hand stopped, she noticed a vellum envelope in it that she hadn't seen when he started the gesture.

"Lord Llyr," he said, "requests the honor of your presence at the duke's ball this coming Friggday."

Annabelle took the letter from his hand. She didn't do it consciously, but the way he held it made it look like he would drop it if she didn't.

"The ball will celebrate and honor the arrival of an emissary from the court of our good King Twilight. There will be dancing, food, and a good time to be had by all."

The messenger paused for a second, but very briefly, as if he didn't want to take the chance that she would say something and interrupt him.

"Lord Llyr will be sending a carriage to transport you to the ball."

The messenger, having fulfilled his duty, turned and moved swiftly back toward his horse. He moved promptly, somehow without giving the impression of rudeness, but quickly enough that Annabelle didn't have time to respond. It struck Annabelle that the messenger didn't want to hear a response in case it wasn't the right one.

She studied the envelope in her hand as the clatter of hooves broke the silence. There was a damp spot on the vellum where the messenger had held it as he handed it to her. Written in large elegant letters on the front of the envelope was her name.

23

Annabelle just stood with the envelope in her hand, even after Bellarose closed the door. It struck her that the handwriting was even nicer than Mr. Miller's. She stared at the pretty swirls and curlicues on the letters of her name. It was her name on the envelope.

"Oh, my," said Mrs. Fisher.

"Annabelle," shrieked Bellarose.

Mr. Fisher walked over to Annabelle. He started to grab the envelope out of her hand, then he took a breath, reached out, and gently removed it. The vellum flap on the back wasn't sealed. He opened it and removed a card from inside.

"Oh, my," said Mrs. Fisher.

Mr. Fisher glowered at the card in his hand. His brow furrowed a bit. "Bellarose," he called.

Annabelle stared at the hand holding the envelope.

"Oh, my," said Mrs. Fisher.

Bellarose walked over to her father. She looked at the card in his hand.

"What does it say, Bella?" he said. "I recognize the duke's seal, but what does it say?"

"Oh, my," said Mrs. Fisher.

It occurred to Annabelle that you could set a clock by her mother's pronouncements.

Bellarose took the card from her father. She handled it like she was touching something that was quite possibly poisonous, and at the same time, was also made of some extremely precious material.

Annabelle waited for her mother to say, "Oh my," again, but she seemed to have stopped to listen.

"His grace the duke, lord of Ardstead and warden of the eastern coast, requests the kind and noble presence of the Lady Annabelle Agatha Fisher ..." Bellarose stopped for a moment, and her eyes grew wide. "Annabelle," she whispered, "you're a lady."

"Keep reading, Bella," said Mr. Fisher.

Mrs. Fisher sucked in a breath explosively. It seemed she had forgotten to breathe since she stopped saying, "Oh, my."

"... At a joyous regale in the regency ballroom of the ducal palace to honor the gracious presence of Lord Taedum, representative of King Twilight of Liamec and emissary from his court. Please attend this Friggday evening at eight o'clock." Bellarose stopped reading. She turned the card over. "That's all it says," she said. "Nothing about Llyr, or a carriage, or anything else."

Mrs. Fisher was breathing again, though her breathing seemed a little labored.

"The invitation is from the duke, for his ball, not from Llyr, though Llyr got him to issue it," said Mr. Fisher. "I'm tired. I'm going to go lie down."

"I'm not going," said Annabelle quietly.

"Oh, my," said Mrs. Fisher.

Bellarose's eyes shot wide open. She looked at Annabelle the way a parent would look at a rebellious child. "You can't not go," said Bellarose. "It's not even an option. For one thing, you don't know how to reach him to tell him you don't want to. For another, he's sending a carriage. And, for a third, you *can't* not go. That's like being invited to go to heaven and saying you want to stay in hell instead."

"It said requests," said Annabelle stubbornly.

Bellarose looked at Annabelle again.

"Mama," she said, "we need to get Annabelle a dress."

24

The wives' circle discussed the problem of the Fishers. It was not a trivial problem and was something the circle was taking seriously. Mrs. Cuttlecutter was not the senior wife at the moment, something that deeply saddened her. Mrs. Bilge was present today, and she exercised her senior duties with diligence.

"When did it start?" said Mrs. Bilge.

"That Llyr coming down the Duke's Way was the first thing that most people saw," said Mrs. Atwater, "but my Dylan says he thinks the sea leaving Chelle was their fault."

"Not sure why that would have been," said Mrs. Cuttlecutter. When she wasn't the senior, she tended to be a little contrary.

"But what about that messenger that came roaring through town like a wave yesterday," said Mrs. Bilge. "My boy said he came down the Duke's Way. And we all know he went to the Fishers, then left town as fast as he came.

"The Fishers have always been uppity," she continued, "just think of that Bellarose. Too good to talk to us, she is." Several of the wives turned to give a look to Elle as she said this. Elle had been keeping quiet on the edge of the circle. She was still, sort of, on probation.

Bellarose and Mrs. Fisher hunted down a dress for Annabelle. Bellarose thought what they found at the market was the most beautiful thing she had ever seen. Mrs. Fisher worried it wasn't good enough, even though it set them back a good part of their savings.

They were in Annabelle and Bellarose's room, and Bella was making Anna wear the dress. "Stand up straight, Anna," scolded Bellarose. "If you walk into the ball slouching like that, you'll embarrass the whole Fisher family."

"Doesn't the color go beautifully with her eyes, Mama?" said Bellarose.

Mr. Fisher abdicated the process to his wife and daughters. He acknowledged that there wasn't any good way for Annabelle to get out of going, though there was nothing else he would prefer.

"I'm a Fisher man," he said, "Fisher men are fishermen. I don't know anything about balls."

25

Friggday afternoon, Bellarose and Mrs. Fisher bustled around Annabelle like bees around a hive. They told her to stand up straight more times than she could remember. At the moment, Bellarose stood behind her, fussing with some straps on the dress. They didn't have a wall mirror. That kind of thing was a luxury that was out of their reach. But Mrs. Fisher had a polished, bronze hand mirror. The two of them tried to show Annabelle how she looked from several angles.

Annabelle kept insisting that she wasn't going to go, but by this time, even she recognized that she didn't believe it. She started to accept what was happening as a sort of doom that hung over her.

As the time when they might expect the carriage to arrive drew closer, Annabelle felt like a condemned prisoner awaiting the executioner. Bellarose and her mother tried to encourage her. Bellarose went back and forth between sympathy and annoyance.

"Annabelle," she said, "you've got to start thinking of this as an opportunity. You're going to be seeing things that people in Chelle just dream about. I'd give all the sea urchins in the bay to be in your place."

Mrs. Fisher was more philosophical.

"It's all right, Anna. Everything that begins, ends."

They heard the clatter of horse's hooves on the rock pathway outside. Annabelle snuck over to a window that looked out onto the stone yard. The carriage, which she could dimly see through a gap between two shutters, seemed so big she couldn't imagine how it had made it down the path.

There was a knock at the door. Bellarose went to answer it. Annabelle's father had gone to the pub.

"Who is it?" called Bellarose through the door.

"Carriage for Miss Annabelle Fisher" came the formal sounding reply. There seemed to be a conflict in the voice between the level of volume needed to get through the closed wooden door and the level that would maintain the amount of dignity that the voice clearly desired to maintain.

Bellarose opened the door. The man who had knocked bowed and moved aside. He was dressed in the livery of a footman. There were three other footmen outside the door. With him stepping back into position, there were two of them standing at attention on each side.

In between the two rows of footmen, was an older woman. She glided forward and lifted her hand toward the inside of the cottage.

"Lady Annabelle?" she said.

26

Annabelle moved forward. There was something she immediately respected about the woman. She was solemn and dressed very elegantly by Chelle's standards. There was a motherly expression on her face, which turned toward Annabelle as soon as she moved.

Annabelle moved forward, and the woman took her hand. They stepped together out into the courtyard. The carriage was almost as large as it had seemed through the slots in the shutters. There were four hanging lanterns attached two to a side on the cabin of the coach. The sky was lit a ruddy orange by the setting sun, and the warm light from the carriage lanterns flooded the stone of the yard.

The footmen standing at attention on both sides of the door were identically dressed in blue. In the warm light flooding the yard, the blue of their liveries glistened in an almost metallic fashion. The four of them looked very much the same, to Annabelle. She wondered if whoever recruited them made an effort to hire men of a similar height.

The carriage was drawn by a team of four beautiful white horses. Annabelle was struck by their similarity to Llyr's horse, Breaker. *They must be siblings*, she thought. The one closest to her nickered fitfully and stamped his forehoof.

"Anna, Anna," came a frantic cry through the cottage doorway. Bellarose came bursting out, holding the envelope containing the invitation in her hands. She thrust the envelope into Annabelle's hands, kissed her on the cheek, whispered, "Good luck," into her ear, and disappeared back into the cottage, all before Annabelle could say a word.

The woman holding Annabelle's hand looked at her again and led her toward the carriage. One of the footmen jumped forward and held open the door. Annabelle raised her foot up onto the running board. She had to lift the bottom edge of her dress to do so. Another woman, almost a twin to the first, was inside the carriage. She leaned down and held her hand out to Annabelle.

As Annabelle took her hand and climbed into the carriage, she felt, for the first time, that this evening might not be so bad. She'd never had so many people eager to help her do anything. The warm evening, the ruddy setting sunlight, the confident faces on the two women in the carriage with her, all combined to give her a feeling of importance and contentment.

That feeling lasted for all of five seconds. As soon as the carriage door closed, the two women looked at each other, nodded, and turned toward Annabelle purposefully.

The carriage started with a lurch and soon made a rumbling sound as the wheels began moving over the rough stone. Within seconds the carriage interior tilted, as the steep ascent up the path from the courtyard began.

The two women in the carriage with Annabelle were being almost eerily silent. They were inspecting Annabelle and seemed very intent on her clothing and hair.

"Is there something wrong?" asked Annabelle. She started to feel self-conscious.

"Of course not, my lady," said the woman who had come into the cottage to get her. "We just need to get you ready."

27

As the carriage rattled and swayed, the first woman reached out to Annabelle and took a grip on her arms. The other one moved around behind her. The carriage was large, but the amount of space inside was still tight. Annabelle felt claustrophobic with the two women so close to her. She tried to see what the one behind her was doing, but the first one had her in a firm grip.

As Annabelle felt the buttons on the back of her dress open, she began to protest. Her protests were ineffective. In short order, the dress Bellarose and her mother dressed her in was lying on the seat beside her.

Annabelle felt like crying. Her sister and mother had been so proud of that dress. The two women looked at her linen chemise, and while they didn't look particularly happy with it, they made no move to take it off her.

As the carriage started rattling along the Way toward Chelle, one woman began fussing with Annabelle's hair. The other opened a compartment above the seats in the carriage and pulled out a gown.

Annabelle got more and more indignant. The silence and seriousness of the two women had cowed her into obedience at first. But the way they were pushing her around was becoming too much. Then she saw the gown.

It took her breath away. She felt like crying again, just thinking about how pleased Bellarose and her mother had been with the dress they had bought. Compared to this, that dress was an inelegant rag. It was a light shade of salmon.

Like the footmen's uniforms, it glistened almost metallically in the patchwork splotches of light that made their way into the carriage interior from the lanterns and the setting sun. Lace and delicate beadwork highlighted the waist and collar—not enough to break the elegance, but just enough to show the gown, and hopefully herself, off in their best light.

"Is that for me?" she breathed.

With no more than a nod, one of the women positioned herself behind Annabelle again and held her arms up. The other one slipped the gown over her head. They bustled and arranged. One worked on Annabelle's hair, while the other made adjustments to the dress itself.

Bothered as she was by the way they were manhandling her, Annabelle couldn't help but admire how competently they were doing it. The carriage rocked and swayed as it clattered along, and Annabelle could hardly keep upright. The two women kept themselves up and managed their work on her at the same time with seeming ease.

When they finished, the two of them sat back and inspected their work. Annabelle felt like something on display for sale at the market. Finally, they seemed satisfied, and it seemed they were done with Annabelle. Once they had finished adjusting the dress, hair, and makeup, they left her to her own devices. They weren't unpleasant to her, they just seemed uninterested. So, she looked around the carriage. The interior was blue in a color that matched the shade of blue of the footmen's uniforms. The decor had a vaguely nautical theme. There were carved wooden seashells, starfish, and seahorses on various surfaces. It was pretty, but not very interesting.

Annabelle addressed one of the women, "Excuse me, ma'am, is there anything I need to know about the ball or the carriage? Will Llyr meet us there?"

The woman turned to her, reluctantly. The smile that was on her face when she escorted Annabelle to the carriage was gone. In its place was a blank expression. Annabelle noticed for the first time how watery her eyes were.

"My lady," she said, "we are just humble servants of the great lord. There is nothing we could say that would be of interest to you." She blinked several times.

28

Annabelle made her way to one of the covered windows of the carriage. One of the women observed her carefully as she moved. She seemed to be keeping an eye on whether Annabelle was careful enough with the gown. At one point, Annabelle reached up to touch her hair, and the woman reached over to her and pulled her arm back down to her side.

They didn't seem to care if Annabelle looked out, however. Annabelle raised the leather flap covering the window. There was a strap attached so you could tie it open.

She leaned out the window. The carriage began to climb the Duke's Way. The sun had set, and a full moon shone on the lane that led back into Chelle. Lit by the moon's light and the glow from the carriage lanterns, Annabelle saw a group of village children watching the carriage as it began climbing. She thought that she saw Jonah among them. Annabelle waved. The children just stared at her.

The carriage rumbled up the Duke's Way. The Way made a series of switchbacks as it wound up the cliff to Ardstead. Annabelle couldn't switch from one side of the carriage to the other easily, the two women were in the way. So, half the time, she had a beautiful view overlooking Chelle and the sea, and the other half all she could see was the rock wall of the cliff.

As a child, Annabelle had climbed partway up the Duke's Way. It was something that the children of Chelle by the Sea did. They would challenge each other to see how far they could get. Some of Annabelle's classmates said that they had climbed the whole way and seen Ardstead, but Annabelle hadn't believed them.

Each time a switchback gave Annabelle a view of the seaward side, she would marvel at how beautiful Chelle looked in the moonlight. Each progressive view gave her a bigger picture of the town. At first, she could just recognize the lanes near the base of the Duke's Way. Then, with the next switch, she could see the market square and the center of town. The following few switches let her look at more and more of Chelle, including the school, the inn, and the houses of people she knew.

The last switchback before the carriage crested the hill let Annabelle see the whole town and the harbor beneath it. For a moment, she thought she could make out her family's cottage on the westward way out of town, but the moon chose that moment to go briefly behind a cloud.

As the carriage crested the ridge and started down the short, gentle slope to Ardstead, the moon peeked out again. Annabelle got one final view of Chelle by the Sea from further above than she'd ever seen it. The lighthouse out on Blindman's Point was lit. She could see the lights of torches around the market square. The bright moonlight shining over the village gave it a glow that warmed her heart. For a moment, she felt sad, like she was leaving home. Then she thought to herself that she was being silly. *I'll just be gone a few hours. I'll be sleeping in my own bed tonight.*

The carriage rolled onward down the short, gentle slope toward Ardstead.

29

Her first sight of the lands above the cliffs glued Annabelle to the window as the carriage rolled toward Ardstead. She noticed how green and lush the fields and hillsides on both sides of the Way were. The cliffs and rock faces that covered everything around Chelle were nowhere to be seen here. The moonlight shone over farmlands and rolling hills.

As the carriage rolled into town, houses started lining the sides of the roadway. The road itself widened and smoothed the closer they got to where people lived. At first, Annabelle wasn't impressed with the sizes of the homes in the town, then they rolled further on, and they kept growing. The houses on the outskirts of town had green areas around them. It struck Annabelle how much green grass and open space each of those homes had.

The carriage rumbled deeper into town. The houses got grander and grander. Annabelle started having trouble taking it all in. As they turned and swayed through the city streets, Annabelle kept getting glimpses of a massive moonlit structure that loomed over Ardstead, as the cliffs below towered over Chelle.

The hill containing the duke's castle, and the castle itself, showed through gaps between the buildings of the town as the carriage pulled toward the town center.

The carriage rolled into a large open square. There was a building that looked like a town hall on one side. On the opposite side was a wide road that rose up the central hill toward the duke's castle. A massive statue stood in the middle of the square. The carriage rumbled into the cobbled square, turned past the fountain, and began the ascent up the hill.

As the carriage went past, Annabelle looked at the statue. It was the figure of Poseidon, his arm upraised, wielding a trident. He held the trident forward, about to thrust it toward something below and in front of him. Being from Chelle, Annabelle was familiar with the different ways Poseidon manifested. As a god, he could appear in various forms at different times. This was the older gray-haired god, stern and mature, representing the god of the sea at his most potent.

As the carriage turned past the statue, there was a moment when the trident's tines seemed to be pointed right at Annabelle. For a second, she felt like Poseidon was about to thrust the weapon at her.

The feeling passed, and the carriage rolled up the hill.

30

The carriage rumbled to a stop in the Inner Bailey of the duke's castle. There were other carriages and buggies of various kinds. Footmen and servants in the duke's livery were milling about. It seemed very busy. A duke's man came forward and held the harness of the lead horse on the team. One of the blue-clad footmen jumped off the footboard on the back of the carriage. He ran around to the door, opening it for Annabelle.

Annabelle looked at the women in the carriage with her. One of them gestured toward the open door. She moved to the door and gazed out on the courtyard.

The castle walls loomed overhead. It was a big open yard, and though the walls were high, it still felt like a welcoming space. The sun had set, and the full moon shone over the battlements on one side of the cobbled yard.

Bright, colorful banners were hung on the walls, and many lanterns were casting a warm light over the entire scene. Annabelle hesitated in the doorway of the carriage. The footman stood below the running board, holding his hand up to help her down.

Annabelle looked at the other guests heading toward the big open double doors that must lead to the great hall of the castle. Ladies and gentlemen. It struck her again how totally out of place she was. They dressed and carried themselves like dreams she had only experienced in her imagination.

Annabelle stood in the carriage doorway, one foot inside, the other outside on the running board. She had to keep her neck bent a little, as the carriage doorway was smaller than a house door. Annabelle felt about to cry. She had never been more out of her element in her life. Her knowledge of how to gut any of twenty different kinds of fish wasn't going to help her here. The footman waited patiently below her.

As Annabelle hovered in the doorway trying to get up the courage to descend, she felt a shove in the small of her back. She grunted and would have fallen headfirst out of the carriage if the waiting footman hadn't caught her. He arrested her fall and somehow even managed to make it look like a simple stumble leaving the carriage instead of a headlong tumble.

Annabelle recovered her footing on the ground below the carriage, with the footman's help, and turned to glare at the carriage door. One of the women looked out. She blinked again, with the same passive expression on her face. Annabelle felt on a more familiar footing. The fear she had been feeling turned to anger. She glared at the woman.

The carriage door closed, and the carriage started rolling on. The footman, standing next to Annabelle, held out his hand to lead her toward the great hall's entrance doors.

Annabelle took his hand, and they walked together toward the large double doors. The footman's grip was a little wet and clammy. Annabelle wondered what he had to be nervous about. He wasn't the one who had to go inside.

31

Her escort led Annabelle through the double doors into the antechamber before the great hall. The doors were wide open, and there was enough space in the entrance that many people were coming and going at the same time.

The antechamber was wide enough that Annabelle became disoriented. Her first thought was there was no way this hallway leading to the great hall could be this wide. It seemed wider than the entire building had looked from the outside.

Then Annabelle was distracted by a woman walking toward the hall as she was. This woman was also escorted by a footman, clad in blue livery like the one accompanying Annabelle. Annabelle was jealous. This woman didn't look out-of-place like Annabelle felt. She was dressed elegantly in a gown that seemed similar to the one the women had put on Annabelle. This woman, however, in contrast to how Annabelle was sure she, herself, looked, looked tall, secure, and beautiful. She wore the dress proudly, and she had hair coiffed charmingly in a stylish fashion. She seemed to fit in here, in a way that made Annabelle even more unsure of herself.

For a moment, Annabelle grew disoriented again. The hall wasn't as wide as it looked. It was walled on both sides with mirrors. Annabelle was looking at herself.

She marveled at the mirrors. She knew the polished bronze mirror her mother had, and she'd once seen a silver mirror, but this one worked better than either of those. She stared at it in fascination. The image in the mirror was so clear it looked real. The footman waited with seemingly endless patience. She focused on the image in the mirror. Her breath stopped. She'd never seen anything more beautiful.

The women had worked on her hair and somehow had time to do something with her makeup. The beadwork and lace on the gown around her throat set off her face exquisitely. The gown's color seemed to complement her dark hair and skin tone like it was tailored for her.

Annabelle didn't recognize herself.

The footman's endless patience had an end, after all. He pulled her onward, leaving the marvelous mirrors behind. They reached the entrance to the great hall, and the man had a whispered conversation with the duke's marshal. Somehow he had gotten hold of her invitation, and she saw him handing it to the marshal. Here, he left her, and the marshal escorted her through the door.

Annabelle did her best to stand up as straight as she imagined Bellarose would want, as she entered the great hall.

32

The lighting was different in the great hall. There were bright lanterns around, especially around the area at the entrance where Annabelle found herself now. There were skylights in the ceiling. Through one, Annabelle saw the familiar presence of the full moon peeking into the grand chamber.

The great hall's entrance area was at the top of a sweeping marble staircase, which led down to the polished central floor. There was a crowd of people lining both sides of the massive room. To Annabelle's right, the elegant ladies and gentlemen were mingling through a buffet of various foods. On the left, they seemed to be gathered in conversational groups. Down at the other end of the hall, it looked like there were more formal events going on. Annabelle caught a glimpse of what might be some kind of throne. Of course, the duke was here.

With the shining lights and being so high above the hall, Annabelle felt like all eyes must be on her. She tried to keep her back straight, like Bellarose and her mother had told her. There were other things they had told her to do, but the lights and the crowd's noises drove them right out of her head. She focused on keeping her back exceptionally straight to make up for forgetting the other things.

Two other people stood at the top of the stairs with Annabelle. To her right was a liveried guardsman, standing at attention. He wore the duke's livery, a dark green tabard with a black silhouette of an octopus. To Annabelle's left was the marshal who had escorted her through the door. He cleared his throat and made as if to speak. Annabelle felt a moment of panic. She'd heard of events where the guests were announced. He couldn't be about to do that to her, could he? She wanted to shrivel up into a little ball and disappear, but she had to focus on keeping her back straight.

"The Lady Annabelle Agatha Fisher," the marshal bellowed. Annabelle wasn't sure how a single human throat could produce a sound of such volume. Half the crowd looked at the staircase, and Annabelle standing there. She felt like the entire universe couldn't help but hear.

Annabelle felt betrayed. First, by the marshal who was pulling her out of her anonymity. Second, by Llyr, who was nowhere to be seen. She also wondered momentarily about the nature of people who wanted to enter a room with so much attention focused on themselves.

Annabelle moved carefully to the top edge of the stairs. She looked desperately for a way to escape the lights and the scrutiny. The crowd to her left was divided into small conversational groups. In one group of five or six younger-looking people, a young woman waved at Annabelle. When she saw Annabelle looking at her, she made a "come here" gesture.

Annabelle made her way slowly down the steps. The last thing she needed was to trip and fall in front of this crowd. She approached the woman who had waved at her. The open floor space in the center of the hall felt like a vast wilderness she had to cross.

As soon as Annabelle was near enough, the young woman pulled her close in a warm embrace.

"Annabelle, I'm so glad you're here. Llyr has told me so much about you. I'm Sibyl. We're going to be best friends."

33

Sibyl released Annabelle from her grip, and Annabelle retreated a step. Sibyl looked her up and down. She smiled. The smile seemed to light up her face and even the surrounding area. Annabelle found herself looking for the shadows cast by that smile.

"You're just as pretty as Pappoli said you were," Sibyl said.

"Pappoli?"

"That's just my nickname for Lord Llyr," Sibyl explained. "It's sort of a joke. He said to tell you that I'm a member of his household. He asked me to keep an eye out for you and make you welcome. Welcome!"

Annabelle looked at the group. In addition to Sibyl, there were three young men present and two more young women. They all looked like they could be within a few years or so of Annabelle's age. They were all looking at Sibyl. They seemed to hang on her every word.

Sibyl was a little shorter than Annabelle, though you wouldn't have guessed it by her presence. She wore a lovely blue gown. Her hair was somewhere between a ginger color and a dark red. Like her smile, the color of her hair seemed to be too shiny and happy to stay in one place. The gown was short enough to be scandalous. Annabelle thought she saw a glimpse of an ankle at one point.

Sibyl continued, without a pause for breath, "Let me introduce you to everyone." She laughed. Like her smile, her laugh seemed full of delight. It was hard to hear that laugh and not laugh, or at least smile, yourself.

"Everyone important that is," Sibyl's smile deepened as she said this. "Annabelle, this is Finley. We call him Fin. He's the duke's nephew." She gestured to the handsome young man standing off to one side. He was tall, and when Annabelle turned to look at him, he almost took her breath away. Black hair like hers, he had chiseled features that looked like they were chipped out of the rock of the cliffs above Chelle by the Sea.

Finley strode forward, took Annabelle's hand, and raised it to his lips.

"Fisher?" he said. "Of the North-gate Fishers? Charmed."

Annabelle didn't want to tell him of which Fishers she was.

"Shut up, Fin," said Sibyl, "You can flap your lips later."

She brought Annabelle's attention to one of the young women in the group.

"This is Evadne," she continued. Sibyl slowed down a little during this introduction. "My ... relative. Evadne is also a member of Lord Llyr's household." In contrast to Sibyl, and the rest of the group who had been sounding very merry as Annabelle walked up to them, Evadne seemed quieter and even, a little sad. She nodded to acknowledge the introduction.

Sibyl waved at the rest of the group. The remaining three young people were eagerly awaiting their turn to be introduced. "These other ones aren't important. That's who you need to meet."

Sibyl continued, "Llyr should be here a little later. He had some urgent business to take care of. Time and tide wait for no man."

34

There was a commotion in the cleared area in the center of the hall. The guests mostly were keeping to the sides. Occasionally, they would cross from the conversational area to the food or the end of the room where the duke was holding court. The commotion was some servants bringing out a chair for a minstrel who was preparing to perform.

Sibyl looked a little bored by this until Annabelle clapped her hands and cried "music," in a pleased voice. Sibyl reluctantly focused her attention on the man approaching the chair.

The minstrel was an older man, by Annabelle's standards. There was a little gray mixed into the brown of his hair around the temples. He wore green tights and a colorful doublet with horizontal stripes of fabric in bright rainbow colors stretched across it. The look made Annabelle's eyes hurt. *Hopefully, he sings better than he dresses,* she thought.

Finley moved next to her. "Annabelle," he said. "That's a lovely name. I don't remember the Fisher family having a daughter your age."

"I'm not one of the North-gate Fishers," Annabelle said.

The minstrel's chair was facing toward the duke's throne, so they were looking at the man from the side. He took a large lute onto his lap and began tuning. The sound of the notes as he plucked each string was already pleasant to the ear.

"What's he going to play?" said Annabelle. She was almost trembling with excitement. Traveling musicians rarely made it to Chelle by the Sea. Finley looked at her with a curious expression on his face.

Sibyl sounded bored. Even with the bored tone, her voice rang out magically and was captivating. "I think it's a new composition. Something about an adventure of the king's. He wrote it to honor the visit of the king's counselor."

"King Twilight?" said Annabelle.

"Of course, King Twilight," said Sibyl. "He's the duke's king, isn't he?"

Annabelle got even more excited. She was very inspired by King Twilight. Mr. Miller had told them about him, but his facts were a little boring. Annabelle preferred the stories that she heard from the peddlers who traveled through town. Even though it was a bit faithless to her family, she enjoyed them more than stories about Caspian Fisher.

"Isn't it lovely the way the notes float across the air?" said Evadne.

Annabelle's favorite story about King Twilight was about how the king had come to power. Annabelle knew about the evil prince regent. How he could turn into a lion at will. How he had tortured people and taxed everyone until they had no money left. The tale of how King Twilight, alone, with just a dagger, defeated him in single combat gave her chills.

Queen Vix was sort of interesting as well. Annabelle sometimes just wanted the queen out of the way, so the king would be free to marry her instead.

35

The minstrel stopped his tuning. He stood and bowed to the duke. Annabelle looked to both sides, and then toward the throne. The crowds had stopped their talking and were paying attention. Apparently, not everyone here was as jaded as Sibyl. Music would still get them to listen. Annabelle was not used to being in a space with this many people. But, as no one was looking at her, she didn't mind so much.

She turned her attention to the duke. This was the first time she had seen him. He had been down to visit in Chelle once when she was two, but her memories of that visit were a little limited. Her first reaction was to be surprised. The duke was a small round man. He was smiling in a friendly, slightly silly way at the minstrel. Even as far away as she was, Annabelle could see that he had a smear of chicken grease on his doublet.

Annabelle turned to look at Finley, who stood not far from her. Then she turned to look back at the duke. *Is there any way they can both be from the same stock?*

Finley noticed her attention and sidled up next to her.

"Is there a family of Fishers in the town of Highland Hill?"

Annabelle just frowned at him, shook her head, and made a shushing gesture with her index finger on her lips.

"Your grace," said the minstrel, "and our most gracious visitors from the royal court," here he bowed again toward a group of people standing to the duke's right. "In honor of the occasion, I have composed a modest piece to celebrate the recent victory King Twilight had over the Ogre of the Etenies. If I may beg your indulgence."

The minstrel sat back down and began playing. He had a soothing voice that didn't sound loud, but somehow still filled the hall.

"The young king stood and faced the morn,
to fear he was a stranger,
No giant vile, nor dragon fell,
would ere our land endanger.

"His land, his people, called for him,
his folk they were in trouble,
A creature dark, as midnight dream,
was laying towns to rubble.

"In the hills, it was, 'tween sea and peak,
his kingdom to the northwest,
An ogre foul, lo ten feet high,
with skulls around its nest.

"The Lady Vix, she pled with him,
to return to her unharmed,
She gave him help, what aid she could,
he went to battle charmed.

"With just a few, his trusted band,
Our king, our lord, departed.
He took no one, he did not trust,
Just bear and wolf, hearted.

"To hunt the beast, they never ceased,
they covered hill and vale,
and in the end, when creature struck,
our heroes could not fail.

"Blow for blow, the king's true band,
matched the creatures might.

J. STEVEN LAMPERTI

The beast was fleet, its strength was vast,
They never thought of flight.

"The battle dark, the fight so ill,
death was barely cheated.
By might of arms, and Vix's charms,
the evil was defeated.

"When day was done, King Twilight came,
The Lady Vix, the bearer.
He gave us life, and brought the dawn,
and evil fled in terror."

36

There was a round of polite applause when the minstrel was done. Annabelle clapped loudly, earning looks from some of the ladies and gentlemen in her vicinity. Apparently, the current fashion was to try to restrain excessive enthusiasm, which perhaps explained some of Sibyl's ennui.

A servant helped the minstrel carry off his chair. He headed over to one corner of the hall where some other musicians seemed to be setting up.

"What's next?" said Annabelle breathlessly. Despite herself, she found that she was starting to enjoy some aspects of the evening.

Finley smiled at her enthusiasm. "I think they're setting up the floor, and the musicians, for dancing."

A group of men was crossing the open floor toward them. It was Llyr, followed by three others, who seemed to be trying to get his attention. Llyr strode aggressively toward the group that Sibyl, Fin, and Annabelle were part of, waving off the men following him like they were annoying flies.

He stopped at the edge of the circle of young people. "Sibyl, Fin, Evadne." As Sibyl, he seemed to know who to ignore in the group. When he said the name Evadne, there appeared to be a measure of deference in his tone.

He reached out his hand, clasped Annabelle's, brought it to his lips, and said, "Annabelle. So glad you could make it."

Like there was any choice, thought Annabelle.

The musicians started playing. Llyr kept Annabelle's

hand in his, gently pulling it and her toward the dance floor.

"If I may have the pleasure," he said with a smile.

Annabelle resisted for a moment, then she allowed Llyr to pull her out toward the dance floor. She didn't get to dance often, and this was a ball after all. She noticed Finley looking after them with a disappointed expression on his face.

Annabelle was relieved to recognize the music and how people were lining up on the marble floor. They were going to start with a circle dance, perhaps to get the dancers warmed up.

There was a weekly dance in the churchyard in Chelle by the Sea. Annabelle and Bellarose often went. When they were younger, much of their time had been spent trying to figure out who was going to ask them to dance. Later, they just started joining the dance without worrying about it.

As Annabelle and Llyr joined the circle, she looked at the dancers surrounding them. There was one big difference between this group and the dancers in the churchyard in Chelle. The clothes and jewelry most of these people were wearing were worth more than the entire possessions of most of her fellow townsfolk.

Annabelle turned to Llyr and whispered angrily, "You abandoned me!"

Llyr smiled at her. She felt there was nothing resembling an apology in that smile.

"I am so, so sorry," he said. "You seem to have done just fine, anyway." It seemed to Annabelle that he was enjoying her anger. She frowned and glared at him.

The pace of the dance picked up, and Annabelle had to focus. It wasn't exactly the same as the circle dances they danced in Chelle.

Annabelle started to lose herself in the dance, the people, the warmth, and the exertion. So what if the gowns the women were wearing could buy and sell Chelle, they were beautiful. The mood was joyous, everyone was smiling and laughing. For a moment, Annabelle remembered what Bellarose had told her.

Here she was dancing on a marble floor in a Duke's great hall with a handsome young man on her arm, even if he was annoying. Whatever would come next, this moment would always be with her.

The circle dance finished. Llyr and Annabelle danced two more dances before they went back to rejoin the others. As she spun, twirled, and hooked arms with the other dancers, Annabelle could feel her cheeks flushing with warmth. Strands of loose hair were starting to sneak their way across her face. She noticed that as she changed partners and locked eyes with the other dancers, the ladies seemed to frown, while the gentlemen seemed to smile more.

Llyr and Annabelle were laughing with the pleasure of exertion as they left the dance floor and walked back to Fin and Sibyl.

37

Evadne wasn't with them. Annabelle looked around for a second to make sure she wasn't just off talking to another group in the conversational islands but didn't see her. She asked Llyr why Evadne seemed so sad.

Sibyl answered. It seemed like she wanted to reinsert herself into the conversation. She'd lost the focus since Llyr arrived.

"Evadne went off to lie down. She was tired. She's got a tragic past." Sibyl laughed merrily at this last line like it was the best joke she'd ever told.

Sibyl grabbed Annabelle's arm and pulled her away from the others.

"Come with me, Annabelle," she said, "I missed you so much."

Still a little out of breath from the dancing, Annabelle looked at Sibyl to see if she was serious.

Fin followed them. He strode up to Annabelle. He smiled at Sibyl as he took Annabelle's hand. Annabelle thought she saw a bit of a smirk in that smile.

"I don't mean to intrude," he said, "but I hoped I could have the pleasure of the next dance."

Annabelle caught a glimpse of Sibyl glaring at the back of Fin's head as he pulled her back onto the dance floor.

Annabelle got lost in the dance again. She twirled and leapt; she sidestepped and pirouetted. Finley kept staring into her eyes with a very intense look. It was a little off-putting. It didn't, however, distract her from the pleasure of the dance.

She was glowing again. She was sure her cheeks were burning red. She worried that she might be glowing a little too much under the arms, but even that didn't stop her enjoyment of the movement and the moment.

The music stopped. Fin and Annabelle made their way off the dance floor. Llyr and Sibyl were engrossed in some intense conversation.

The duke's marshal, the same one who had introduced Annabelle, stepped forward, just to the right of the duke's throne. He cleared his throat extremely loudly to interrupt conversations and draw everyone's attention to himself.

"Lord Taedum, the chief minister of our good King Twilight, graces us with his presence."

Annabelle was impressed again with his voice. He seemed to fill the vast hall with sound effortlessly.

She was excited. Here was someone who had actually met King Twilight. This man she was about to see and hear had seen the king, spoken to him, and spent time with him. She felt like she was in a fairy tale.

Lord Taedum stood and walked over to where the marshal stood. He bowed to the duke, and then to the gathered crowd. Even before he said a word, Annabelle felt like there was something wrong. Sibyl held her hand over her mouth to hide a yawn. The man practically exuded boredom.

He was tall, and not terribly bad-looking in his own way, but that was where the positive thoughts Annabelle could think about him ended. His hair was a pasty blond color mixed with gray. His face was long and looked dour. As he opened his mouth to speak, it seemed like even he wasn't interested in what he had to say.

Mercifully, after he was done talking, she thought of another positive adjective to apply to him: brief. He spoke for just a few minutes. Afterward, she couldn't remember a word he had said. It'd been something about being happy to be there and keeping the lines of communication open between the crown and the duchy.

Annabelle turned to Sibyl, who had stood next to her as they both tried to stay awake during the counselor's words.

"How can he be from the court of King Twilight?" Annabelle said. "He's the most boring person I ever heard."

Sibyl laughed. Annabelle felt her heart melting in Sibyl's direction again. The sound of her laugh was so infectious.

"Annabelle," she said, "That's what kings, courts, and counselors are. Boredom."

38

When Lord Taedum finished speaking, the floor was cleared, the musicians resumed, and Llyr asked Annabelle to dance again. The whirl and swirl of the dance steps and the dance floor's bustle intoxicated Annabelle once more. She started losing track of time. As she tried to stop to take a break, one of the young men whom Sibyl had dismissed earlier pulled her back out onto the floor with a wink and a smile.

Annabelle was flushed and happy. She felt like the belle of the ball. She lost count of the number of times she tried to leave the dance only to be pulled, encouraged, asked, or begged to return. At one point, she thought she saw Sibyl regarding her with a sour-looking expression on her face. But her features vanished into a parade of faces that Annabelle locked eyes with while moving on the marble surface of the ballroom floor.

Eventually, she had to stop. She was feeling tired and hadn't eaten anything. She fought her way through the dancers and over to the spot where their group had been standing. There was no one there.

Annabelle was reluctant to make her way across the dance floor to the buffet by herself, so she looked around to see if she could find anyone from her party. She found one of the unintroduced young women, who indicated a doorway on one side of the ballroom. She said that she had seen Sibyl and Finley heading in that direction.

As Annabelle approached the doorway, she heard voices. Momentarily overcome with shyness, she stopped by the door and peered furtively around the doorframe.

Sibyl and Finley were with a group of young people around the minstrel, who was sitting on a divan, his lute on his lap.

"Sing us one of those Twee songs," said Sibyl merrily.

"Officially, I'm not supposed to know those," said the minstrel with a wink. He looked around theatrically and said, "My apologies to the red queen." His fingers began to move over the strings of his lute. Annabelle was once again enchanted by the notes from the instrument and the sound of his voice.

"A young man named Twee was in Grisput one day,
he met a young maid, who wouldn't say nay.
He asked her her name, and she didn't reply,
She just made a sound, much like a sigh.

"He vixed her, he vaxed her, I'm sad to say he vexed her.
He fixed her, he taxed her, he had to unhex her.

"A young man named Twee was on his way to Cap,
he saw a pretty maiden and sat her on his lap,
She wiggled so sweetly, he gave her a little kiss,
She looked at him sternly, and said 'please sir, more than this.'

"He vixed her, he vaxed her, I'm sad to say he vexed her.
He fixed her, he taxed her, and then he had to flex her.

"A young man named Twee was fighting with a lion,
He saw a pretty maid, who seemed to be cryin',
He said, 'Pretty maiden, what seems to be the trouble?'
she answered, 'Kind sir, my nettle bed is rubble.'

"He vixed her, he vaxed her, I'm sad to say he vexed her.
He fixed her, he taxed her, and lastly, he perplexed her."

39

Annabelle had mixed feelings about the song. She really enjoyed the musician, but the words didn't sound very respectful to the king and the queen. There was a murmur of appreciation from the crowd of young people. The trill of Sibyl's laugh rang out afresh.

Annabelle peered around the doorframe again. The crowd was breaking up. Sibyl and Finley were heading toward the doorway she hid behind. She was embarrassed she was spying on them and started to hurry away before they saw her. Then, she heard them talking and made out her name.

"Well, that was fun," Finley said, "Shall we try to find Annabelle?"

Sibyl laughed once more. "Why would I want to spend any more time with that peasant fishwife? She's stupid, and she smells like seaweed."

Annabelle felt her heart dropping out of her chest. For a moment, this was her worst fear coming true. They knew who she was and that she didn't belong here. For that same moment, she felt like a fraud, like fleeing the ballroom in tears.

Then, surprisingly quickly, her sorrow turned to anger. *Who were they to think they were better than she was. She came from a village where people worked for a living. These people sat up here in their fancy castle on their fancy hill and lived off the work of others.*

Annabelle left her hiding spot behind the doorframe before Sibyl and Finley could see her. She looked for, and found, another hallway leading out of the ballroom.

Annabelle felt her anger growing as she ran blindly through the corridors of the castle. She hunted down hallways, looked through doorways, peered up staircases, looking for any way out of the duke's stone edifice, which felt oppressive and heavy overhead to her now.

Annabelle dodged servants, avoided corridors that seemed like they were leading back toward the ballroom, and finally found an open archway that appeared to be leading outside. She walked through the arch and into a garden.

The full moon shone down on the scene in front of her, lighting up plants, pathways, and arbors. She sniffed the air and smelled the sea. More distant than she'd ever felt it in Chelle, but the smell of the sea nonetheless.

The garden lined the seaward side of the castle. It was lit by lanterns, perhaps for the ball guests' pleasure, though no one other than Annabelle seemed to have found their way out here.

Annabelle raced along a pathway through the garden to a low stone wall that bordered a cliff overlooking Ardstead below. She stopped at the wall and looked out at the moonlit scene. Ardstead was luminous in the moonlight. The glows in the windows of many houses, combined with the full moon's light, made the town look magical. She could see beyond Ardstead to another cliff edge that must be the drop-off above Chelle.

Even their town is prettier than ours, she thought angrily.

Beyond the further cliff, Annabelle could just make out a light that must be the Blindman's Point lighthouse.

"Annabelle," came a quiet voice from behind her. She turned and saw Llyr walking up toward her.

"What do *you* want," she said. Annoyance dripped from her voice.

40

Llyr tilted his head to one side and looked at Annabelle calmly. "Was it something I said?" There was sympathy in his voice, and this time he sounded sincere. Annabelle felt her anger ease a little. Or at least shift its direction away from Llyr.

"Not you, no," she replied.

"Sibyl, then," said Llyr, "that girl doesn't know how to play nice."

Annabelle didn't respond, but it seemed that her silence spoke volumes.

"I'll have a talk with her," said Llyr. This time it was his turn to sound annoyed. "She needs to learn how to get along with people."

"It's not just her," said Annabelle. "I shouldn't be here. This isn't my place. If you wouldn't mind, I'd like to go home."

Llyr looked disappointed. "It's still early. I can make Sibyl behave," he said.

"This isn't my place," Annabelle said again. "These people don't know anything about what it means to sweat for a whole day and smell like fish guts."

"Should they?" asked Llyr, with a slight frown.

"Mr. Miller has been teaching us some things that the town council probably wouldn't appreciate," said Annabelle. "He's read to us from Plato's Republic, and talked about the connection between Chelle, Ardstead, the fishermen, and the duke."

Llyr said slowly, "Has he, now?"

"The riches of Ardstead, the duke, this whole castle and

town, are based on the work of my town's people. My fellow citizens do the work, and these people profit."

Llyr looked thoughtful. "That doesn't sound right." It was like the thought had never occurred to him. "The people of Chelle are closer to the sea."

Annabelle started getting excited about her subject. "We need some better way to make things work. They're living off our backs!"

Llyr nodded. He looked at Annabelle like he was seeing her for the first time. "You know, Annabelle," he said, "I think you've got a point. I'll have to do something about that."

Annabelle stopped talking and just looked at Llyr.

Llyr continued, "I never really thought about the economics, but I agree that they're selfishly profiting off the workers of Chelle."

"They?" said Annabelle. She looked at him. "You're one of them."

Llyr stood up straight. His teeth clenched. He looked bigger somehow.

Annabelle took a step backward. Llyr's shift in mood made it feel like the ground was shaking. She felt a little unsteady on her feet.

"I am not one of them," said Llyr. Annabelle had never heard anyone say something in a tone that made it more apparent how important it was to them. Llyr wasn't shouting, but it felt like he was. His voice sounded louder than anything she had ever heard without actually being loud. The sound of his words was filling the gaps in the air between all the leaves on the trees and all the grass blades growing on the ground. "You have no idea who I am!"

41

Llyr was breathing heavily. Annabelle watched him, somewhat like you might observe an injured animal to see if it was still dangerous. Llyr's breathing slowed. He calmed. He seemed to Annabelle to shrink as he did so.

"Let me take you home," he said. "If you don't mind, though, I'd like to make one stop first. I didn't get a chance to eat, are you hungry?"

Annabelle realized that she was. In fact, she was starving.

Llyr took her hand and led her through the garden. There was a path through the gardens that led back to the Inner Bailey. They didn't have to reenter the castle. Annabelle was relieved. She didn't want to encounter Sibyl again.

When they got back to the Inner Bailey, the carriage was waiting for them; though, Annabelle didn't really feel like it was waiting for her. It was waiting for Llyr. If she had tried to come out here without him, she didn't think it would have been here.

Llyr helped her up into the carriage. He climbed in after and sat opposite her. There was no sign of the ladies who had accompanied Annabelle here. She wasn't sure if the footmen were the same or not. They had looked a little similar to each other and still did.

Llyr reached up and rapped on the roof of the carriage. Annabelle felt the rumble as it started rolling over the cobbles of the courtyard. Llyr leaned toward her attentively and said, "I'm sorry if the evening's entertainment wasn't to your liking." When he focused his attention on her, it was hard to remain angry. In fact, it was hard to think about anything else except what he was saying.

"I enjoyed the dancing," Annabelle said. As she said this, she realized that she really had. She'd enjoyed it more than she had anything in years. Anything, since Corentin had died.

"I'm glad," said Llyr. He leaned back and seemed to relax a little on his side of the carriage.

Annabelle looked out the window on her side. They were rumbling quickly through the streets of Ardstead. The moonlight cast a friendly glow on the houses, but she was less interested in the sights than she had been on the way up.

Just as it was hard to not listen when Llyr spoke, it was easy to join him in silence. The two of them sat in a companionable quiet for some time. The carriage made its way through Ardstead and then began the long descent into Chelle.

"What did you mean, you'd have to do something?" ventured Annabelle, as the carriage rolled down the bottom of the Duke's Way. "It's not a problem that one person can solve."

The carriage reached the bottom of the Duke's Way and turned to the right. Annabelle slid over to the window and looked out.

"We're going the wrong way," she exclaimed. "Our house is in the other direction!"

Llyr smiled. "Like I said, one quick stop first. I promise you won't mind."

Instead of proceeding through Chelle, past the town square, to the Westward Way and her family's house, the carriage wound its way through the other side of town and to the Eastern Way. They turned off the Way onto a side road right before it started to climb into the cliffs to the east of Chelle.

The carriage rumbled to a stop, and Llyr helped Annabelle out. She knew the road. They were at the side of the track that led to the lighthouse. The footmen were all bustling around, several held torches. Llyr took Annabelle's hand again and led her toward a trail that went up a low hill. With one footman behind, another in front, and two more carrying something, they proceeded up.

When they reached the top of the hill, the footmen laid down a travel rug and opened the baskets they were carrying. Llyr gestured to the carpet, swept one hand theatrically in front of him, and said, "My lady."

42

Annabelle took in the view. They were looking down on the road that wound out to Blindman's Point and the lighthouse. For a moment, Annabelle wished she could fly. The glowing moonlight illuminated the lands of the Blindman's Point Peninsula. The fields and rolling hills between where they were and the lighthouse looked soft and rounded in the crisp light. There was a gentle breeze blowing just a trace of chill into the air. Annabelle shivered.

Llyr immediately removed his cloak and placed it over her shoulders.

"If you'll have a seat," he said, "I think you'll enjoy this."

Annabelle noticed the smells coming from the baskets. The footmen opened them up, set up a couple of lanterns for light, and then withdrew.

Annabelle tried to figure out how to sit on the travel carpet in her gown. This was a kind of challenge that she hadn't had to face before in her life. Llyr watched with an amused smile on his face.

Eventually, she managed and looked into the nearest of the baskets. They were filled with seafood delicacies. Not really a surprise, considering where they were. The smells coming out of the baskets made her mouth water. She really was hungry.

Llyr started serving. He seemed to know each dish intimately.

Annabelle had eaten seafood her entire life. Of course, in Chelle, it was what there was, and everything else had to be imported. The people of Chelle, though, cooked quite plainly. The art of the chef was not regarded as highly in Chelle as in other places.

Annabelle had tried dishes from Ardstead. In Ardstead, the culinary arts were prized, and especially the preparation of seafood. It was what they added to the work of the people of Chelle, and though there were questions about the division of labor, what they did, they did well.

This food, however, put the work of the best cooks of Ardstead to shame. Each dish was exquisite. Each flavor matched with the others flawlessly. Llyr knew what to give Annabelle, and when. He knew which dish would complement another. There seemed to be little cooking involved in the preparations.

Annabelle had never tasted the things her father caught each day prepared so delicately. It was like the cooks had a relationship with each fish. Like they knew each one personally, and so knew best how to prepare it.

When they had finished eating, they sat back on the carpet for a moment and enjoyed the moonlight.

"That was delicious," said Annabelle. "I'm full. I couldn't eat another bite."

"I'm glad," said Llyr with a smile. "Let me take you home."

43

The morning dew was still lingering on the cobbles of the street. The streets in Chelle by the Sea usually glistened in the early morning, as the sun tried its best to break through the clouds and turn the gray skies blue. The moisture was a combination of fog and sea spray.

A man was walking down the street. A big man. Heavy and solid looking. He was a presence, not one of those men who can walk down a street and be ignored. There was a happy smile on his face. His walk was light and tripping, surprising in a man of his size.

He wore a dark blue shirt and brown pants, both made of fine material. He hummed a bit as he walked.

The man stopped for a moment, lifted his head, and sniffed the air. A range of emotions sprinted across his face. Chelle often smelled like the sea. In the morning and the evening, the smell of the sea was at its purest. During the day, it was diluted by the activities of the folk of the town. In the morning and the evening, before and after people did things which added to the smells, all you could smell was the sea.

The smell of the sea on the coast is, in some ways, the smell of death. A fish decomposing on the beach, mussels that seagulls have lifted to great heights and dropped onto rocks to get at the meat inside, and seaweed exposed to more air than it would like. There are also the smells of life, but the smell of the place where the sea meets the land contains death. The dying of the sea stranded on the shore.

The emotions that flitted across the man's face recognized this. He sorrowed for the death in the smell; he gloried in the life. He reveled in the excitement of the waves crashing onto the shore. The parade of emotions ended with the happy smile that it started with. In some ways, that smile seemed too happy. A reasonable man, thinking about the state of the world, might find it hard to have that expression on his face.

Jonah was up early. Some mornings he ran down to the sea for a quick dip before helping his father get the boat out for the day. After that, many days, he had school while the fleet was out. Jonah looked forward to next season when he would join his father on the boat. Jonah was dressed, defying the morning chill, in just a breechclout and leather sandals.

The man walking into town down the Eastern Way, the boy running from his home toward the sea, saw each other and stopped. Even if Jonah hadn't seen that the man was coming into town down the Way, it would have been clear that he was a visitor to Chelle by his clothes, if nothing else.

The big man dropped a deep bow to Jonah.

"My lord," he said. "If I might beg a favor of the man who will best the king of the sea?"

"Um ...," said Jonah.

"A boon, a favor, I am in need of direction."

Jonah sighed. "You're looking for Annabelle, aren't you?" he said.

The big man looked startled. He dropped his bow even further and pressed his hand to his forehead.

"I have mistaken you," he said, "You are a prophet, or perhaps a small god, to be so wise in the ways of the future. Forgive me, my lord."

Jonah shook his head. He was very uncomfortable with this whole situation.

"Everyone who comes to town nowadays is looking for Annabelle."

44

The man looked confused for a second, then his furrowed brow cleared. "She has roused the interest of Lord," he hesitated a second then continued, "Llyr. People are interested in who Llyr is interested in." He smiled. The smile looked too simple for a man who seemed to be saying nonsimple things. "That's why I'm here, myself."

"I can take you to her," said Jonah. By the time they got to the other side of town, Annabelle would most likely be leading Soggy to market. He frowned for a second and said, "Why do you want to see her, anyway?"

"My lord," said the man, "I would be forever in your debt. I am one of those who remember debts. As far as why goes, I assure you my intentions are entirely honorable. I am Llyr's brother and only want to meet the object of his interest."

"Brother?" said Jonah. "Older brother?" He looked at the man critically. By his best guess, this man was somewhere in his forties. He was showing just a trace of gray at the temples and was starting something of an ale belly. Llyr looked barely older than Annabelle.

"Older, younger. Is the mind older than the sea? Is a bush older than a tree? Is a lyre older than a song? Is right older than wrong?"

Jonah frowned again. "That's not an answer."

The man looked confused for a moment. "It's not?"

Jonah started off down the street toward the other side of town and Annabelle's house. The man followed. He seemed to lose focus as they walked. He started looking around at things they passed. At one point, a stray cat crossed their path. It darted from a side alley, across Market Street, the street they were traveling down, and down another alleyway.

The man startled as the cat entered the roadway and tracked its path with rapt attention. He moved as if to follow it down the alleyway. Jonah cleared his throat and pointed down the road toward the market. Shaking his head, as if to clear his thoughts, the man followed.

As they crossed the still mostly empty marketplace, Jonah tried to engage the man in conversation.

"So, where are you and Llyr from, anyway?" he asked.

"Well," the man paused, and seemed to take this question seriously. "I guess I'm from Llyr, and he's from me. And, I think, we're both from our father. But aren't we all?"

"Huh," said Jonah. He again didn't think the man had answered his question, but it was better than the awkward silence they had been sharing.

"Though I guess you could say that I'm not really his brother. I might be his nephew. His father and my father might really be his brother if you know what I mean."

Jonah was confident he had no idea what the man meant and became more confident with each word.

They crossed the market. Jonah greeted Ondine Shoaldraught, who was helping her mother unload the family cart. They started down the lane that led toward the Fisher's home. The man kept talking.

"My father, who I said was his father, who might really be his brother, and wants to be yours, by the way, helped him be born. That's what a father really is, isn't it?"

Jonah, relieved to see Annabelle leading Soggy down the lane, said, "There she is!" He pointed Annabelle out to the man and raced ahead to give her a warning.

"Jonah," Annabelle said calmly as he ran up to her.

Jonah leaned close to Annabelle and, breathlessly, let an unpunctuated stream of words flow into her ear.

"Annabelle this man says he's Llyr's brother I've gotta go need to help my father with the boat he wants to talk to you careful I think he's barmy."

He turned and fled back down the lane.

45

Annabelle was leading Soggy to market without Bellarose. Bellarose had woken this morning with an upset stomach. She complained to Annabelle, and Annabelle relayed the message on to their parents. When she told them, they looked at each other and nodded sagely.

"Bad fish," said their father meeting the eyes of his wife.

"Bad fish," she replied.

They weren't referring to what Bellarose had eaten the night before. Though, that might have been the source of the problem. "Bad fish" had become what people in Chelle by the Sea said to each other when something went wrong. When two townsfolk passed on the street, an overheard conversation might go like this: "Looks like thar's some weather blowing in from the Noreast."

"Bad fish."

As Annabelle watched the large man dressed in his dark blue and brown ambling toward her, she muttered under her breath, "Bad fish."

Halting the mule and taking a tighter grip on his lead, Annabelle waited as the man walked up to her and bowed.

"Annabelle Agatha Fisher," he began.

"Why does everybody know my middle name?" said Annabelle.

The man paused for a moment, looked thoughtful, and said, "I can't speak to why everyone knows it. I can only address why I do."

"So. Why do you?"

He looked even more thoughtful. "I'm sorry, my lady. I have no idea."

He started again. "Annabelle Agatha Fisher." He paused, looking askance at her to see if she was going to interrupt again. Reaching up to sweep his hat forward in a graceful gesture as part of the deep bow he was making, he realized he didn't have one on. He finished the gesture anyway with an imaginary hat in his hand. "I am known as Koalemos, but I would be delighted if you would call me Cole."

"What can I do for you, Cole?" said Annabelle.

46

Cole looked at Annabelle and began speaking. "It is of importance to the world at large, but especially to the sea, what Llyr does." He hesitated again when saying the name Llyr. It seemed like saying that name bothered him for some reason.

"All right," said Annabelle, slowly.

"He has taken an interest in you," Cole continued. "That makes you interesting."

"Nothing else?"

"Pardon me?" said Cole. His hand fell to his side. It seemed that he dropped his imaginary hat.

"Nothing else makes me interesting?" said Annabelle.

"Uh ..."

"I see," said Annabelle. Lifting Soggy's lead, she started walking on toward the market square.

Cole came hurrying after. "Pardon me, my lady, we seem to have gotten off on the wrong foot."

Annabelle stopped Soggy again. "Well, show me the other one, then."

"The other one, my lady?"

"Foot, the other foot," said Annabelle impatiently.

Cole looked at her. The smile that had seemed locked on his face was gone. He looked a little sad and bewildered. Annabelle felt sorry for him for a moment.

"My lady," he said, "I am but a simple man. Unwise in the ways of the world, and unsophisticated in verbal duels. If you give me just a moment to tell you why I am here, it would mean more to me than a droplet of water to one parched in the desert."

"All right then," said Annabelle, "say your piece."

Cole looked confused again for a moment. It seemed that he might not have thought this far ahead.

"My lady," he began. A noise from down Market Street interrupted him. Both Annabelle and Cole looked up. It was the clattering sound of horse hooves on cobbles. Llyr was riding quickly toward them.

He pulled up Breaker's reins right beside them, and the horse came to a graceful stop. Soggy shied away from Breaker. Llyr dismounted quickly and smoothly.

Despite herself, Annabelle found that the presence of the man, and horse, moved her. He was young, strong, and handsome. It was hard not to be impressed with the smooth grace with which the dismount was executed. And Breaker's beauty hadn't lessened since she last saw him.

"Koalemos," said Llyr with a frown, "must you?"

"Cole," said Cole with a sullen look downward.

47

Cole looked up from the ground. "You've done this before," he said, "and it's never worked out well for anyone." He had the air about him of a petulant child. Annabelle looked back and forth from one to the other. This had the look of an old argument between siblings, but she had no idea what they were talking about.

"Cole," said Llyr gently, his voice suddenly filled with family concern. "won't Campe be looking for you? You don't want to give her reason to worry, do you?"

Cole shivered. "I don't like it down there," he said, "it's dank and gloomy. I like it much better out here." He made a sweeping gesture that seemed to take in all of Chelle, as well as the sea and sky.

Llyr turned to Annabelle, leaned toward her, and said, "Annabelle, I'm sorry you had to see this. I'm afraid, my brother ..." He hesitated a moment, then continued, "... cousin, is a little off." Llyr tapped his temple with his index finger. "He is cursed with idiocy and prophecy in equal measure."

Llyr hesitated again, looked thoughtful for a moment, and said, "Well, I suppose he may have more of one than the other. I'm really not sure."

"I must warn you, Annabelle," said Cole, "My Lord Llyr is not who he seems. The heavens above and the heavens below beseech you to take care."

"That's entirely enough out of you," said Llyr. He took Breaker's lead, grabbed Cole's arm, and started pulling both of them down the road away from the market square.

"I'm sorry your way to market was interrupted, Annabelle," Llyr said.

Cole turned and, as best he could with Llyr holding his arm, while being dragged away, gave Annabelle another bow.

"Delighted to have met you, my dear," he said. The smile that had left his face for a bit was back. "I see what he sees in you."

48

Llyr and Annabelle were out in Annabelle's vinscif. The sky was the usual gray, though today, it was in a good mood. The sky and the winds accommodated Annabelle's desire to have a calm trip and avoid excitement.

They had left from the dock on the small harbor below the Fisher home. Annabelle was desperate to find something to do to entertain Llyr. He seemed unwilling to leave her alone. Her parents, and especially Bellarose, wouldn't let her say what she wanted, which was telling him to take a long run on a short pier.

When Annabelle had suggested a sail in her vinscif, Llyr was very receptive. He said that there was nothing he enjoyed more than sailing in a small boat, the wind at his back, and the salt spray in his face. This sounded so much to Annabelle like a sentiment that she might have expressed herself that she momentarily gave him a suspicious look.

They had sailed from the dock to the town harbor, through the cliffs guarding the harbor entrance and into the open ocean. They sailed past the breakwater on the western side of the harbor entrance and skirted the coast. The lighthouse and Blindman's Point were to their left.

Annabelle could make out the buoys that showed where the Widow-maker Shoal started below the point. She thought she could see the Petcher family's new boat past the buoys. Hamish Petcher still wasn't listening to the advice of his fellow fishermen.

"Bad fish," Annabelle muttered to herself under her

breath.

For a while now, Annabelle and Llyr had sailed in companionable silence. The quiet felt relaxed and comfortable. *He's almost bearable this way*, thought Annabelle.

Llyr seemed to take Annabelle's muttered words as an invitation to speak.

"Annabelle," Llyr said. He hesitated as if he was unsure how to continue. She took her attention away from the tiller for a moment and looked at him. In her, admittedly limited experience with him, she hadn't seen Llyr unsure of himself too often.

"Annabelle," he continued, "I have a confession to make."

Annabelle looked around the deck of the small boat for something she could use as a weapon. *Here it comes*, she thought.

"I'm not who you think I am," said Llyr.

"Who do I think you are?"

"It doesn't matter. I am not that person. I am Poseidon, king of the sea!"

Llyr stood in the vinscif facing Annabelle and looked stern as he pronounced this. He almost seemed to be glaring at her.

Annabelle dropped the belaying pin she had picked up. It fell with a mild clunk into the bottom of the boat. She started laughing. She laughed so hard that she momentarily lost hold of the tiller. The boat wavered in the wind and began to come about. Llyr staggered briefly. Annabelle grabbed the tiller again and took control of the vinscif before it shifted enough in the wind that the boom swept across the deck, taking Llyr with it.

Llyr looked angry. Being laughed at was obviously not something he enjoyed. He stood taller. Clouds moved across what sunlight there was, and the day became grayer still.

"I am," he said plaintively.

"Of course you are," Annabelle said. She tried to figure out the quickest way to take the boat back home.

49

Llyr remained standing in the boat. *If he were really the king of the sea*, Annabelle thought, *he would know that you don't stand in a vinscif this size without holding on to something.* She thought for a moment about swinging the tiller to one side and trying to knock him off the boat with the boom.

Llyr continued glaring at her. "I will have to show you, then," he said.

He lifted one arm dramatically, then raised it above his head with a sudden gesture. The clouds moved even closer around the sun, darkening the already gray sky. The wind picked up. A set of white-capped waves rose from the ocean, surrounding the vinscif, creating a formation around them. The waves were traveling in the same direction the boat was moving and almost seemed to be escorting it. Llyr dropped his arms to his sides.

Annabelle kept her hand on the tiller and looked to both sides, startled. She'd never seen the ocean behave like this. For a moment, she felt betrayed. She felt like she knew the sea as well as anyone, loved it as well as anyone. How come she'd never seen this side of it?

"Not enough?" said Llyr. He lifted his lowered hand again and held it out toward the nearest wave, making a beckoning gesture.

The wave moved closer to the vinscif. It seemed to move on top of the water instead of being a part of it. The other waves followed in their formation.

Llyr lifted his outstretched hand upward. The white caps

of spray on the tops of the waves rose out of the water, forming into beautiful white horses. The vinscif was being escorted by a dozen glorious white horses, galloping on top of the water. As Annabelle watched, several of the horses turned their heads toward her. They seemed aware of her presence. One shook his head, waving his brilliant white mane in the wind.

    The nearest of the horses was Breaker. Annabelle wasn't sure how she recognized him, but she did. He galloped over near the boat, pushed his head against Llyr's hand, and acted just like Soggy would when he wanted Annabelle to give him a carrot.

    Llyr lowered the outstretched hand back toward the water. The horses settled back into waves, then the waves settled back into ruffled ocean.

50

Annabelle brought the vinscif into a little cove that lay just below the lighthouse on the end of Blindman's Point. The boat was sheltered from the wind, and she lowered the sail. After bringing down the sail, she sat down on the gunwale and started shaking.

Llyr came over to her, looking solicitous. She scooted away from him on her seat on the side of the boat.

"Annabelle," he said, "it's all right. I'm still the same person."

"It's not all right," she said, "You're not the same person. Are you even a person? What did you mean, Poseidon? You're some kind of wizard or something."

"I'm not a wizard," Llyr said. There was an element of disdain in his voice. "I am Poseidon, lord, and ruler of the waters."

Annabelle started crying. Llyr just stayed where he was for a moment, obviously unsure what to do.

Annabelle sniffed. "If you're really Poseidon, I ask you again, like I asked you before. Why are you here?"

Llyr stood again. No hand raised to the heavens this time, he just looked at Annabelle and spoke.

"It was for you, Annabelle, it was all for you. I took the sea from Chelle because of how the town was treating you. They didn't appreciate you. They didn't see how you were connected to the sea. Your father didn't see how you were from and of the sea. He took your brother, who obviously had the land in his soul, to the sea instead of you. Your town doesn't see the beauty of a woman with the oceans in her eyes."

When Llyr mentioned her brother, Annabelle's sniffing stopped.

"It was for you, Annabelle. I saw your connection to the sea from beneath the waves. I saw your love for the oceans each time you sailed your vinscif. Loving the sea is loving me."

Annabelle looked at him thoughtfully.

"It was for you, Annabelle. It was all for you. I loved you from afar before I ever met you. I loved you from beneath. I loved you from above. I was in the waves that splashed over the gunwale of your vinscif. I was riding Breaker across the waters near you the first time you went sailing on your own. I was clinging to the bottom of your hull the last time you sailed the waters. What woman wouldn't want the love and attention of a god?"

"Well," said Annabelle, when Llyr paused for a breath. It was Llyr's turn to stay quiet for a moment. "I can think of a few," continued Annabelle. "Leda, Callisto, and Demeter."

Llyr looked a little disconcerted. He started to speak, "Uh..."

Annabelle continued, "Alcmene, Persephone, Medusa..."

Llyr held up his hand. "All right, I get the point. You have to understand, those were different times. Also, most of those were my brother, not me. He can be a bit of a scoundrel."

Annabelle stood up and started to raise the sail. "We're going home. I need to think about this."

"Whatever you need," said Llyr.

51

Annabelle and Llyr walked along the rocky beach below her house again. She hadn't tried to tell anyone what he had told her. Even Bellarose, though Bellarose had insisted on hearing every detail about the sailing trip. There was no way they would believe her, and she wasn't sure how to even begin to tell it.

"So," said Llyr, "have you thought about what I asked you?"

"You didn't ask me anything."

"I thought the question was implicit in my declaration of love," said Llyr.

"So, Poseidon, huh?" said Annabelle.

"Yup," said Llyr.

"As in, the god Poseidon. Brother of both Zeus and the lord of the underworld. Son of Cronus. Married to Amphitrite?"

"Well," Llyr hesitated as if thinking how to respond, "Amphy and I are going through a bit of a rough patch. We're seeing other people. But, otherwise, pretty much."

"And, Cole?"

"He called himself my brother, but to tell the truth, everyone kind of lost track of exactly how he's related to the family. Nephew would be fine, I think."

"Well," Annabelle began, "family is very important to me, being a Fisher, and all."

"Of course," said Llyr.

"I'd need to know more about yours and probably meet some of them before I could even consider getting closer to you."

"You've met Sibyl and Evadne. Some of my children. Who else would you want to meet?"

"My father always said, 'Judge a man by his brothers.' Maybe I could meet one of your brothers?"

Llyr paused. "Zeus is really quite busy, and Hades doesn't get out much."

"Well," said Annabelle, "You've already mentioned that Zeus is a scoundrel, so it'll have to be your other brother, the lord of the riches from under the earth." It was considered very bad luck to say Hades's name out loud. Annabelle shivered when she heard Llyr say it.

"As I said, he doesn't get out much. I'm not sure I can convince him to leave the underworld to come up here for a visit."

"Well, then, we'll have to go see him, won't we," said Annabelle decisively.

52

Annabelle's family was under the impression that Annabelle and Llyr were just going walking again. Annabelle's mother, thinking it might be a long walk, packed Annabelle some sliced bread and cheese, wrapped in wax cloth.

"There's enough there for two if Llyr wants some," she said. Annabelle just gave her a look.

Llyr came by on Breaker, and Annabelle met him in front of the house.

Annabelle dressed as best she could for travel. Nowadays, her mother frowned on her wearing pants. She had a traveling skirt that was cut a little shorter, and she wore some linen leggings underneath it. She wore a cambric tunic and had a shoulder bag strapped on over one shoulder. That was where she was carrying the bread and cheese her mother had given her.

Llyr dismounted smoothly from the horse, took the lead in one hand, Annabelle's hand in the other, and started walking back up the slope toward the Westward Way. It was a lovely morning, for Chelle, and walking with the girl beside him, leading his horse, seemed like a pleasant way to enjoy it to Llyr.

"You won't leave me, will you?" said Annabelle.

"Leave you?" said Llyr.

"In Hades. I know that this was my idea, but it's scaring me now."

"I won't leave you," said Llyr.

"Promise. Promise me you won't leave me. By all the stars in the sea. Promise me you won't leave me in Hades."

They reached the top of the climb from the courtyard.

Annabelle looked back at the little yard around her home. The iron hooks that she and Bellarose hung laundry on made her feel like crying for a moment. Her mother came out and headed toward the garden the family maintained in one corner of the yard. She looked up, saw Annabelle looking down, smiled, and waved cheerily.

"Don't you mean all the stars in the sky?" said Llyr.

"Of course not," replied Annabelle.

"I promise," said Llyr, "by all the stars in the sea, I promise I won't leave you in Hades."

53

Jonah hid behind some large rocks on the side of the Way. He had followed Llyr out to the Fisher house. It bothered him how much time Llyr and Annabelle were spending together. This morning, especially, had given him a bad feeling. He tried to keep close enough to the two of them as they walked so he could see where they were going without them seeing him.

"Can't you just snap your fingers and get there instantly?" said Annabelle.

"I could," said Llyr, "but you're mortal, and there are rules and procedures that have to be followed. You have to do things the right way."

Llyr released Annabelle's hand. They walked side by side, with Breaker following just a step behind. He kept bumping his head against Llyr's shoulder every few minutes, in case somehow Llyr should suddenly come up with a carrot or apple that he hadn't come up with before.

The sun continued its eternal battle with the habitually gray skies. Today in an unusual sign of strength, the sunshine was managing to peep through the clouds. Perhaps Helios was keeping an eye on his cousin. The warm beams of sunlight caressed Annabelle's shoulders.

"I know a shortcut. It won't feel that far," said Llyr. He continued to lead them along the Western Way away from Chelle by the Sea.

Jonah was getting a little nervous. He had no idea where

Llyr was taking Annabelle. There was nothing out of Chelle on the Western Way for leagues. If they were trying to go anywhere on this road, they should be riding Breaker, not leading him.

They turned a corner. The cliff face rose above them on their left. Annabelle knew the area well. She, Corentin, Bella, as well as other friends from Chelle, had played here as children.

There was a cave opening in the rock face just around the corner. Annabelle stopped in shock and stared at it. There had always been a large recess in the stone on the side of the Way here, but it didn't go very far back into the rock face of the cliff.

"This isn't here," she said quietly. "There is nothing like this here."

"Don't worry, Annabelle," said Llyr with a smile, "I'm with you." He gripped her hand again and led her and Breaker into the cave.

Jonah turned the corner after them just in time to see Llyr, Annabelle, and Breaker disappear into a cave that wasn't there. It was there for a moment, then it wasn't. Jonah ran forward into the recess at the side of the Way. He stared at the rock wall in front of him.

"Annabelle!" he cried.

54

The cave was dark. As they went away from the opening, it got even darker. Annabelle felt the comforting grip of Llyr's hand, but the darkness quickly made her nervous. It was also warm and close, and she had no idea where they were.

"Just a moment," said Llyr. Annabelle heard him mumbling, and half saw, half felt him put the hand that wasn't holding hers on Breaker's side.

The horse began to glow—a soft glimmering light, reminiscent of the light cast by the moon on a night when it was full. The light illuminated the cave. Breaker stood proudly, almost as if he knew that he was providing a service by lighting the area. Also, almost as if he knew how well the light showed him off. His white sides and mane shone majestically. He looked a horse fit for a god to ride.

Annabelle looked around. The cave was low but just wide enough for the three of them to walk side by side. She looked back but already couldn't see the entrance behind them. The floor under her feet was paved with flat flagstones. The cave seemed to stretch forward into a tunnel.

"Where are we?" she said.

"This," replied Llyr, "is one of the paths to Hades. I've heard it said that a new flagstone is laid down on this path whenever a good person dies. One of my brother's decorating ideas. Sometimes I think he's a little too clever for his own good."

"How far is it?" said Annabelle. Despite her best intentions, now that they were on their way, she was nervous. She kept a tight grip on Llyr's hand.

"That's hard to say," said Llyr with a chuckle. He seemed to find the question amusing.

They walked on in silence for a while. Breaker's glow lit the walls of the tunnel, which continued unchanging. The flagstone path had a small downward incline, which gave Annabelle the feeling that they were descending, but it wasn't anything resembling steep. She quickly lost track of time.

At one point, they stopped for a breather. Llyr pulled a blanket out of one of Breaker's saddlebags, folded it into a pad, and placed it on the flagstone floor for Annabelle.

"Do you mind, Annabelle?" he said, "I've got an errand to run. I'll be back in a trice." He smiled at her, made a big show out of snapping his fingers, and faded out of existence.

Annabelle stared. She tried to figure out how she had gotten into a world where this kind of thing happened. She sat down on the blanket, pulled one of the cheese breads her mother had given her out of her shoulder bag, and started munching on it.

Breaker came over to her and pushed his head against her shoulder. She looked a little deeper in the bag, found an apple, and gave it to him.

Soon enough, Llyr returned. Annabelle couldn't have said how long he was gone. She and Breaker had shared a quiet moment.

They walked further down the tunnel.

After a while, the tunnel opened up into a spacious cavern. Lit by smoky torches, this larger cave seemed like some kind of gathering place, though there was no one there.

Llyr stepped forward, turned to Annabelle, bowed to her, and said, "Welcome, my lady, to the gate to Hades."

55

The cavern was large but completely empty. The top of the cave was high enough that Annabelle could barely make it out. On the opposite side from where they came in, was a stone archway over another tunnel mouth.

Llyr led Annabelle and Breaker across the cavern toward the archway on the other side.

"Annabelle," he said, "you realize that this will put you into a very select crowd." He looked at her and raised one eyebrow.

Annabelle looked at the stone-carved lintel over the tunnel mouth they were heading toward. There were words carved into the lintel, though she couldn't read them.

"Is that Greek?" she asked.

"Yes, of course," said Llyr. He continued his thought. "Heracles, Theseus, and of course, Orpheus. And now, Annabelle Agatha Fisher."

Llyr looked thoughtful for a moment. "Though," he said slowly, "they are known for coming back. You haven't done that yet. Lots of mortals *enter* Hades."

"What does it say?" said Annabelle.

Llyr waved one hand dismissively. "Oh, something about abandoning hope if you enter. I don't bother looking at it. I certainly don't bother abandoning any hope."

He looked thoughtful again. "Though," he said, "that's true for me. You are mortal, after all. You might want to abandon a bit of hope."

The cave felt dry, well lit, and the air felt relatively fresh as they walked across. It surprised Annabelle.

"I thought of Hades as misty and dank," she said.

"We're not in Hades yet," said Llyr. "After we enter that archway, we are officially, but there's still a way to go to my brother's palace."

Llyr slapped one hand to his forehead. "By my marrow," he said, "I forgot. Do you have any money?"

"A little," said Annabelle, "how much do you need?"

"One coin will do," said Llyr, as they moved on through the archway.

56

They walked down another tunnel. It didn't seem like a long walk to Annabelle, though it didn't seem short either. She found herself unclear how far they traveled. The tunnel walls were smooth, and unlike the path to Hades, the floor of this tunnel seemed to be cobbled, not paved with larger flagstones.

Llyr, Annabelle, and Breaker came out of the tunnel mouth onto a vast open space. They stood at the top of a slope that descended gently down to what looked like the shores of a river below. The air was clear and a little chilly, though Annabelle could see what looked like fog rolling along the banks of the river.

The sky was gray. Familiar to Annabelle, in some ways, the firmament and the lighting reminded her of the gray cloudy skies that hung over Chelle. There were no clouds, but she couldn't see either blue sky or any kind of ceiling. Gazing up, all she could see was a featureless gray. As she watched, she saw a flock of birds flying by. Inspected a little closer, they looked like some kind of reptiles.

There were mountains and hills in the distance in several directions. Annabelle could see other rivers winding through valleys, and nearby, a wider one meandering through a canyon. The path that came out of the cave curved gently down the slope below them to the river embankment.

There was a trace of sulfur in the air—just a hint, not enough to be unpleasant.

The slope of the hillside below them, and as far as she

could tell the rest of the nearby hills, were carpeted with blue-gray grass. She didn't see any trees.

"Magnificent, isn't it?" said Llyr.

Annabelle stayed silent, taking in the surrounding sights.

"My brother certainly has a nice realm," continued Llyr. "That's the Styx below us. That river making its way through the canyon over there is the Lethe."

He gestured as he spoke. He seemed to enjoy showing Annabelle the scene.

"Elysium is over there, just past the Phlegethon." Llyr motioned off to their right.

Annabelle looked over in that direction. Far off in the distance, she made out an orange line and beyond it, bright light shining on green fields. Squinting a bit, the orange line resolved itself into a flowing stream or river of flame.

Looking back at the waterway below them, she could just make out what seemed to be some buildings on the other side. Llyr saw where she was looking.

"Those are the Halls of Judgment. We can skip those." He winked at her. "This time."

57

They started down the paved path toward the river. Annabelle looked at Breaker to see how he took to the unusual conditions. He seemed completely unfazed. She reflected for a moment on the fact that it wasn't just his beauty that made him an unusual horse.

The path wound around a hill, and the riverbank came into view. There was a boathouse and a dock at the end of the trail. A small brown punt was tied up alongside the landing. It was clear to Annabelle that this was a ferryboat, and their next step would be ferrying across the river.

As Annabelle, Llyr, and Breaker approached the dock, they heard a nasal rumbling, whistling sound coming from the boat. It reminded Annabelle of some of her father's worse night noises.

Llyr walked over to the boat and looked inside it. Annabelle thought she saw a momentary flash of distaste appear on his face. He rapped sharply with his knuckles on the side of the punt.

There was a groan from below the gunwale. A tousled head of greasy gray hair appeared above the edge of the ferry, followed almost immediately by the most intense blue-gray eyes Annabelle had ever seen. The eyes felt like they were looking through her when they turned in her direction.

A small man stood in the boat, climbed out, and stepped onto the dock next to them. He was a little shorter than Annabelle. Dressed in a grimy gray tunic and ripped leggings, he looked like he hadn't bathed in several moons, even though he was sleeping in a boat on a river. He had an uncombed beard, matching the gray hair on top of his head. Somehow, he managed to combine gaunt skin stretched over tight cheekbones with a belly that pushed out on his tunic.

"Charon," said Llyr coolly, "I thought you would be working the Acheron instead of the Styx."

"You need something?" the man said equally coolly. He turned his intense gaze on Llyr. It surprised Annabelle to see that Llyr's face didn't burst into flame with those eyes pointed at him.

"What do you think we need?" said Llyr.

Charon turned his gaze on Annabelle. He held out his hand toward her. She scrambled to get her shoulder bag open.

"Uh," she said, "how much is it?"

"One coin," Charon replied. His voice was just a little gentler speaking to her. "It doesn't matter what kind."

She fumbled a coin out of her bag and put it into his palm. She tried to avoid touching the hand, as the grime that he seemed to have rolled in covered that as well.

Llyr made a move toward the ferryboat. Charon moved between him and the punt and held out his hand toward Llyr as well.

Llyr looked shocked.

"Are you kidding me? You know who I am!"

"Rules is rules," said the boatman.

After flashing an angry look at Charon, Llyr turned to Annabelle.

"I promise I'll pay you back," he said.

Annabelle pulled out another coin and handed it to Llyr, who passed it on to Charon.

The two of them climbed into the small ferryboat, followed closely by the ferryman. They found a place to sit somewhere in the middle of the punt.

Charon climbed onto a platform at the back of the punt, untied the boat, picked up a pole that must have been three times as long as he was tall, and pushed the ferry out into the mist covering the river.

58

The ferry eased slowly out into the shallow waters of the river. Mist shrouded the riverbanks. Soon there was nothing to see but the boat, the surrounding water, and the ferryman pushing with his pole. The quiet sound of water rippling around the pole and splashing against the boat sides was the only thing they heard. The smell of sulfur was a little stronger here on the water.

Annabelle broke the quiet. "What was that errand you went on?"

"Oh, just that thing you asked me to do," said Llyr.

"I haven't asked you to do anything," replied Annabelle.

"Oh," said Llyr. "think of it as a gift, then."

"You make a lot more noise than the dead," said Charon disapprovingly.

Annabelle suddenly felt her face growing red. *I can't believe we forgot*, she thought.

"Breaker! We forgot Breaker!" she cried. She had an image in her head of the horse standing patiently and watching as they got onto the ferryboat.

"Not a problem," said Llyr calmly. He stood up, and the boat rocked a little. Charon gave him a dour look. Annabelle was glad that he wasn't glaring at her.

Llyr faced back toward the dock. He lifted one hand and made a beckoning gesture.

A white-crested wave came toward the boat over the surface of the river. Without wind or other waves, it looked entirely out of place. The ferry rocked again as the wave took up a position next to it. Llyr sat back down.

Charon used his pole to steady the boat. "A lot more noise," he said, shaking his head.

59

A matching dock on the other side of the river pulled into view out of the mist. Charon maneuvered the boat alongside it. The white-crested wave had kept pace with them the whole way. There was a small clunk as the ferry's side bumped up against the wood of the pier.

Charon stepped out of the punt and tied it up on the dock. Llyr and Annabelle climbed out. Llyr turned toward the wave that had traveled alongside the boat and made one more gesture. Annabelle watched with amazement as the wave crashed onto the riverbank, the white foam crest rose out of the water, and Breaker danced onto the shore.

Llyr turned to the ferryman. "Charon," he said. The man just grunted and turned back toward his boat.

The path they were following on the other side of the river continued on this side. Breaker walked over to them and pushed his head affectionately against Llyr's shoulder. When Llyr didn't respond, Annabelle dug through her shoulder bag and found another apple.

As soon as they left the riverside, the mist cleared up. The path they were on went into a narrow canyon between two hills. It felt shadowy and dark. Annabelle wondered where the shadows and the light were coming from without a sun in the sky.

Her thoughts were interrupted by a surge of noise and action from her right. Out of a dark cave mouth in the cliff on the right side of the path came an angry dog. Growling, barking, and snarling, all at the same time, it charged toward them.

It took Annabelle a moment to take in what was happening, and another moment to believe what she saw. The dog could growl, snarl, and bark all at the same time because it had three heads. The creature was at least as high as her shoulder and standing on its hind legs would have been taller than she was. At the point where its shoulders joined its neck, the neck split into three. Each one of the three heads glared angrily at her.

Llyr stepped in front of her. The dog pulled up abruptly. One of the heads tilted to one side and gazed at Llyr quizzically, another looked confused, and the third started sniffing at him.

Annabelle took a step back.

"Cerberus?" she said.

"Of course," said Llyr. He reached out toward the head that sniffed at him, holding his hand palm downward, below the head's nose.

The dog's tail, which was surprisingly long and somewhat snake-like, started whipping back and forth like a metronome. The head that was sniffing began bumping up against Llyr, pushing its nose into his midriff. The confused one drooped a little and looked like it might be about to take a nap. The last head popped up into an alert-looking position and turned toward Annabelle and Breaker.

Llyr put his hand on the head that was pushing its nose into him. He started stroking an ear. "Who's a good girl?" he said. "Did you miss me?"

60

Annabelle walked forward gingerly. The head that had looked sleepy snapped to attention and turned toward her. The other two were busy occupying both of Llyr's hands. Its teeth bared, the head growled at her hesitantly.

Annabelle slowed and put her hand forward carefully, palm downward, as Llyr had, for the dog to sniff. "Good doggy, Good Cerberus," she said.

The growling stopped. The dog first sniffed at Annabelle's hand, then reached out a long tongue and licked it.

Llyr was still occupied with the other heads. The dog's snake-like tail lashed back and forth so furiously that Annabelle was a little scared.

The other two heads grabbed hold of Llyr's tunic with their teeth and started gently pulling. The one in front of Annabelle watched her curiously.

The dog pulled on Llyr. Leading him toward the cave.

"Do we have a minute for a byway, Annabelle?" said Llyr. "I think she wants to show me something."

Cerberus pulled Llyr, with Annabelle and Breaker trailing after, into the cave. Once she saw that he was following, she released his tunic, and trotted on ahead, looking back with one head to make sure he kept up. The cave walls were rougher than the tunnels they had traveled through.

The light from the cave entrance was getting dim as they approached what looked like a kind of nest. It was a pile of old clothing that the passing dead must have dropped or lost as they made their way through the canyon. There were fancy satin surcoats mixed with fur stoles. There were beggars' rags and garments that wouldn't have looked out of place on a king. The pile of abandoned garments was heaped up against one wall of the cave. A couple of stalagmites kept it from spreading across the floor and held it in the nest shape.

Llyr moved forward and looked over the edge of the nest. There was an odd snarling, yipping, groaning sound coming from the nest that made Annabelle nervous.

"Annabelle," Llyr said, "come here, you've got to see this."

Annabelle walked to the edge and looked carefully over the side. On the floor of the nest, lying, rolling, scrambling on the cast-off garments of queens, thieves, scholars, and beggars was a wriggling hoard of puppies.

Annabelle tried to make sense of what she saw. There were six, nine, ten, no, three puppies in the nest. Each of the three puppies had three heads, which was what made counting them a chore.

The puppies noticed Annabelle and Llyr. They started scrambling up the side of the nest toward them. Like their mother, each head did something independently from the others. The chorus of small barks, yips, whimpers, and yelps produced a wild cacophony. They looked young. They were still stumbling a bit as they walked. The first of the three tried to make its way up the side of the nest, slipped, and tumbled back down, taking the other two with it. All three wound up back where they started on the bottom of the nest.

Annabelle looked startled for a moment. She stared at a part of the nest. She reached in and pulled out a piece of cloth. Llyr was still looking at the puppies and didn't seem to notice. Surreptitiously, Annabelle stuffed the scrap of fabric she had picked up into her shoulder bag.

Annabelle wasn't too familiar with dog breeds. There weren't many dogs in Chelle. There wasn't much hunting to be done on a fishing boat, and most of the people in Chelle by the Sea were too poor to need or be able to feed a guard dog. From what she did know, however, it looked like some of the puppies had heads from different breeds. The lead one, who had rolled his or her siblings back down to the bottom of the nest, seemed to have one poodle head, another that was a spaniel, and a third that was a greyhound.

Llyr turned to Cerberus, who was looking over the edge of the nest with them. He reached out and patted her on a head.

"You dog, you," he said.

61

Annabelle, Llyr, and Breaker walked on down the canyon path that led from Cerberus's cave. After a little happy puppy playtime, they left Cerberus when the puppies grew insistent on nursing.

Annabelle felt sorry for Cerberus. When the puppies thought it was time to eat, they got very demanding. The chorus of puppy noises grew louder. As Cerberus lay down to let them latch onto her nipples, Annabelle only saw two rows of four.

The canyon opened out into a meadow of the same gray-blue grass that carpeted the hills. It was short and didn't seem like it got any longer, but it didn't look unhealthy even though it wasn't green. It looked like that was just the way it grew.

The road they were on continued straight toward some distant buildings. They turned off that road before they left Cerberus's canyon too far behind.

"This is a shortcut to the palace that won't go by the Halls of Judgment. It's crowded over there, and you wouldn't believe the complaining," said Llyr.

They followed a little dirt path that led up into the hills from the side of the main road. For the first time, there were signs of human habitation other than the Halls off in the distance. Annabelle saw shacks, tents, and what might be small clusters of buildings off to the side of the path they were traveling.

"There are people living here," she said with excitement.

"Living?" said Llyr.

As they rounded a turn, they came across a person at the side of the path. It was an older woman, sitting on a low embankment, staring somewhat blankly ahead of herself. She responded when Annabelle greeted her.

"Hm?" she said and turned in Annabelle's direction.

62

The woman was a little older, perhaps Annabelle's mother's age. She looked at Annabelle as if she looked through her for a moment, then she blinked, seemed to focus a bit, and said, "How can I help you, dear?"

She wore a smock of homespun cotton, with a colorful hat on her head. The bright colors in the hat brought out the pallor in her cheeks. She looked like she hadn't seen the sun in years. Annabelle looked at the sky and thought that probably she hadn't.

It wasn't just pallor from lack of sun, her skin looked a little bluish, almost translucent. She looked like she'd been sick.

"Are you all right?" said Annabelle.

"Of course, dear," said the woman. "Aren't you a pretty one." She reached out a hand and stroked Annabelle's cheek. Her fingers were bluer than her face and felt icy cold.

Annabelle shrank back from her touch. The woman looked sad.

"Was there something you needed, dear?" she said.

Llyr gave Annabelle a look. It was clear to her that he was trying to tell her she was wasting her time.

"My name's Annabelle. Who are … were? You?"

Llyr stepped a little further down the trail. Waiting for them to resume their journey.

The woman looked confused for a moment. She raised one blue finger to her chin. She hesitated as if trying to come up with an answer to the question.

"I'm not sure I remember," she said. "I'm waiting for the

results from the Halls of Judgment."

"How long have you been waiting?" asked Annabelle.

The woman looked at her as if the question were silly.

"Since I got here, of course," she said.

As they walked further on, Annabelle talked to Llyr about what she had heard.

"That was sad," she said. "How long do you think she's been waiting?"

"Time is what it is. Here, sometimes, it is what it isn't," said Llyr. "Some people get through quickly, some are stuck for a while. When they're fresh, they're more lively. Though even then, lively might not be the right word. Sometimes they complain. After a while, they get like that." He looked thoughtful for a moment. "It might have something to do with the river Lethe, known as the river of forgetfulness. It's not too far from here. For some of them, it might be a blessing."

As they kept on walking, they encountered more people. All of them had the same bluish translucent pallor Annabelle had seen on the old woman's face. Many had similar vacant expressions.

63

The trail wound up into the hills, then down the other side. They followed it for a long time. As they descended toward a valley below, Annabelle started thinking it might be time for a break.

"Don't you have another errand to run?" she asked Llyr.

"Always," said Llyr. "You want some alone time?"

There was a pretty, tinkling stream paralleling the trail, and they were just passing through a small grassy spot carpeted with the blue-green grass and edged with gray boulders.

"I'm a little tired, and this looks like a nice place to rest."

"I do have a few things I could take care of," said Llyr thoughtfully. He snapped his fingers again, and Annabelle and Breaker were alone.

After looking around to make sure Llyr was really gone, Annabelle sat on a boulder. She cupped her hands, filled them from the stream, and took a refreshing drink of the cool, clear water. Then, she pulled the piece of cloth she had found in Cerberus's nest out of her shoulder bag and spread it out on the rock in front of her.

It was stained, torn, and partly covered in wiry puppy fur, but she was sure it was Corentin's scarf. The same one he had worn on his last day on earth. Looking at her brother's scarf, Annabelle was overcome with monumental grief. She started sobbing.

The fishermen of Chelle by the Sea often wore scarfs to protect their necks and faces from the sun and the wind. Annabelle's mother had made this one for her son to keep him safe and healthy while he was out on the fishing boat with his father.

Annabelle couldn't stop crying. It was like she was grieving for her brother all over again.

Llyr reappeared. He faded gradually into existence like a person approaching on a foggy night. He had a self-satisfied smirk on his face. The expression changed to concern when he saw Annabelle crying.

"Annabelle, are you all right?" he said. He took in the scene. "You didn't drink water from that stream, did you?"

Annabelle turned her tear-stained face up toward him.

"That's a tributary of the Acheron. The river of sorrow and pain. That's not good." Llyr produced a folded pocket-handkerchief from somewhere and wiped a tear off Annabelle's face.

"The Fates don't like it when a living person drinks from the Acheron. But, the drinker's not usually the one who dies." Llyr shook his head.

"I forgot to tell you to be careful what you eat or drink down here," he said ruefully. "A little late now, I guess."

Annabelle sobbed again. She felt like she wasn't just grieving for her brother, but for someone else as well.

64

The mountain trail rejoined a more extensive road that ran through the bottom of a valley. The valley sides loomed overhead on both sides of the broad way. Even without trees, the rocks and crags made it hard to see what was around the next turn. They headed to their right when they left the trail and joined the road.

There were more people here. Both walking along the road and going about their business in buildings and on paths on both sides. Annabelle tried to get some sense of what that business was, but it was hard. Some of them seemed very busy and purposeful, and others seemed distracted and vacant. All of them shared the same bluish translucence.

Annabelle still sniffled a bit. The sadness that had overcome her was fading slowly, but fading to a dull ache, not ease. She felt like there was some fresh grief there, not just the old wound of her brother's death.

She tried to distract herself by observing the inhabitants of Hades. She looked carefully from side to side, scanning each face with care.

"They're not that interesting," said Llyr. "For the most part, their time of being interesting is done."

It was because she was carefully looking at faces that she recognized the duke, even though she had only seen him across a crowded ballroom floor. He walked past them on the other side of the broad roadway.

Annabelle intercepted him.

"Your grace," she said with a curtsy. His face shared the

bluish tint of his fellows.

The duke nodded his head in acknowledgment. He maintained his round figure, though the rosy complexion she had imagined on his features was missing.

"Do I know you, Miss?" he said, with a friendly, encouraging smile. He seemed more energetic than most of the people they had walked past. This must be what Llyr had meant by "fresh."

"I was at the ball you gave for the king's envoy," said Annabelle. "Just a few days ago. I'm surprised to see you here. Did something happen?"

"I'm sad to say, Miss, but I'm afraid I drowned. A sad business." His brows knitted.

"I'm so sorry," said Annabelle, "how did it happen?"

"My nephew Finley and I were out for a pleasure sail in our cog, the Duke's Buoy."

He winked at her. "He's my heir, you know. Because I have no children of my own.

"The storm was very unexpected. The sailing master told us that there were red skies the night before, and only fair sailing to come."

Annabelle felt a moment of grief for Finley. He had been very charming to her on the dance floor.

"Sorry again, your grace. How goes your judgment?"

"I'm very hopeful. It's onward to the Fields of Elysium for me!"

65

The road wound on through the hills and valleys of the underworld. Annabelle wondered for a moment why they didn't ride Breaker. He was certainly strong enough to carry both of them. But, Llyr seemed to be contented with the three of them walking side by side, so she didn't bring it up.

At first, there were buildings lining the route, and paths and side roads leading off in different directions. People were going both directions on the main way, and often on the side streets. Then, the surroundings changed. On the left, Annabelle saw trees for the first time here in the underworld. A vast orchard opened up, with rows of trees stretching as far as the eye could see. They looked like fruit trees to Annabelle. On the right was a fenced-off field of the same blue-green grass they'd seen on the hills. Annabelle spotted some cattle off in the distance.

"We're getting close," said Llyr with satisfaction.

"The fruit?" said Annabelle.

"Pomegranates. For some reason, my brother really likes them." Llyr replied.

The sound of a distant trumpet blast shattered the air. The people traveling the road walked, ambled, or shuffled, depending on their liveliness, to the sides of the way.

"What's that?" said Annabelle.

"We're in luck," said Llyr. "That has to be a royal procession. Not sure where he's going, but my brother doesn't travel light. Now we won't have to walk the rest of the way to the House of Hades."

As she had before, Annabelle shuddered when Llyr mentioned his brother's name. It was a name everyone knew, but you were supposed to be careful when you said it for fear of drawing the wrong attention.

They moved to the side of the road. Breaker drew looks. Annabelle realized that she hadn't seen any horses or mules among the crowd.

They stood under the canopy of one of the orchard trees. A ripe pomegranate hung just over Annabelle's head. She started to reach up toward it. Llyr looked at her and shook his head.

As the procession reached them, Annabelle had to agree with Llyr. His brother certainly didn't travel in plain company.

First to come down the road were three, winged women. It struck Annabelle how things could still amaze her. She would have thought nothing could, after the things she had seen. These three women had young, strong-looking bodies, but the withered faces of age. They flew low over the road, the tips of their birdlike wings striking the cobbles. They wore boots, leggings, and tunics of black leather. Each bore a whip. They scanned the faces in the crowd as if looking for someone, anyone, who deserved a lashing.

As they flew by Llyr and Annabelle, one of them seemed to meet Llyr's gaze. Annabelle wasn't sure, but she thought she saw a wink.

"The Furies," whispered Llyr.

Following them was a tall, pale man dressed in flowing black robes. He was accompanied by a large number of small, winged men and women flapping around him like a flock of birds. The wings on these little people looked bat-like. The man himself was lost in thought. It didn't look like he knew or cared where he was.

"Morpheus and the Oneiroi," said Llyr. "Don't look at him too closely, or you'll see him later in your dreams." Annabelle averted her gaze.

66

Next to come marching down the road were two relatively ordinary-looking people. It surprised Annabelle to see how normal they looked. Llyr seemed almost more interested in them than he was in the others. He named them as they walked by.

"That's Menoites, the herder. I'm surprised he's not out in the fields. Ascalaphus. He manages the orchard."

Annabelle started to lose interest. *How can I be bored watching a procession of gods?* She thought.

The next three were more interesting. They walked in a row and held themselves sternly upright as if showcasing their authority.

"The judges," said Llyr, "Minos, Rhadamanthus, and Aeacus. Aeacus is also my brother's doorkeeper."

Interesting combination of jobs, thought Annabelle, *doorkeeper and judge of the dead.*

"No wonder it's taking so long to judge everyone," she said, "if they're always out walking in parades."

"Hermes, Hecate, and Hypnus," said Llyr. Annabelle didn't notice who he was talking about, because Hades's chariot had come into view.

It was glorious. Golden and pulled by four horses black as a starless sky. The horses were an inverted image of Breaker. *It can't be real gold*, thought Annabelle, *otherwise, it'd be too heavy for the horses to pull it.*

The horses were trotting proudly down the road. Their

heads were lifted high as if they were honored to be pulling this particular chariot in this particular place.

On the chariot, standing as straight and proud as his horses, was Hades. He was tall, dressed in a gray mantle. He held his bident scepter in one hand and the reins in the other.

Now that's what a god is supposed to look like, thought Annabelle.

He looked older than Llyr. Old enough to be his father. Though Annabelle knew the gods could manifest themselves in different forms.

His head was covered in thick curly black hair streaked with silver-gray. A well-kept beard of the same colors swept down to just above the waist. His gray mantle draped over one shoulder and across his chest. It was fastened around the middle with a belt that glinted gold, matching the chariot. A massive key ring covered with keys hung from one side.

His face looked stern and unforgiving. He certainly looked like a man you wouldn't want to cross. Annabelle understood, looking at him, why people were careful not to say his name.

Cerberus stood beside Hades on the back of the chariot. One head was pressed up against Hades's gray-clad leg. The other two watched the dead lining the roadway.

How did she get here before us? Annabelle wondered.

The chariot pulled up next to where Llyr and Annabelle stood. The stern-faced god riding on the back nodded his head to Llyr and said, "Brother."

67

Hades climbed down from the chariot and walked over to them. Annabelle had gotten used to Llyr. With his casual manner, she had begun to feel at ease around him. Hades radiated power and authority. She felt awed by his presence.

Cerberus bounded off the chariot and raced over to Llyr. She started rubbing her heads up against him. Hades frowned at her.

With the chariot stopped, the procession marchers moved off to the side of the road. The marchers out of the way, the dead resumed their business. A steady flow of walking, ambling, shambling blue-visaged people proceeded by in both directions. Even with what was happening in front of her, Annabelle tried to keep an eye on their faces.

"Brother," repeated Hades, "may I ask your business in my realm?"

"Of course," said Llyr, "I should have let you know I was coming."

The contrast between the young man with his youthful, vibrant stance, and the older mature looking god, standing tall and stern with a slight frown on his face, couldn't have been more striking. If you looked past the visual contrast, you could see from the body language that this was a meeting of equals.

"This," said Llyr, "is Annabelle Agatha Fisher." Hades turned to look at her.

Annabelle flushed and tried her best to curtsy. It wasn't a gesture she was very comfortable with or needed to use often.

She was sure it wasn't as graceful as Sibyl would have managed. Though, probably, Sibyl wouldn't have been as awed by the company as she was.

Hades turned to Llyr and, half under his breath, but still loud enough that Annabelle could hear, said, "One of your conquests, I suppose?"

Llyr made a shushing gesture, one finger to his lips.

Annabelle bobbed her head toward Hades, and said, "Pleased to meet you, my lord."

"Brother," said Hades, "you know how little I like to see the living down here amongst my flock." He swept an arm across the crowd passing by on the road. "Is there any reason I shouldn't strike her down now and have her join them?"

Annabelle shrank back. She took a step sideways as if to move behind Llyr.

"She is here under my protection, under my guidance. I have made her a promise that she shall return to the surface world. And so she shall."

68

Hades walked back to his retinue. Llyr was trying to reassure Annabelle that she wasn't about to join the blue-visaged dead. "His bark is worse than his bite," he said. "Unlike this girl." He rubbed one of Cerberus's heads between the ears. The other two pushed up against him, seeking the same attention. "You really don't want her to bite you."

Annabelle was shaking. She felt that she had really overshot her bounds. *It'll all be worth it, if only ...*, she thought.

"I'll go talk to him," said Llyr. "I'll see if I can get him to listen." He walked over toward where Hades was engaged in conversation with members of his entourage.

With the procession halted and the crowds moving again, more underworld inhabitants were passing by than before. Left to her own devices, Annabelle resumed scanning the features of everyone walking by. She stopped, focused on one face in the crowd of people. "Corentin!" she cried.

Annabelle rushed over toward the crowd.

It was Corentin. Her eyes hadn't been deceiving her. He looked exactly the same as he had on the last day she saw him, except for his missing scarf. He hadn't aged a day. He had been a year older than her. Now, it looked like she was a few years older than he was. Corentin was her older brother; she had looked up to him. Now, she found herself the taller of the two.

She pulled him from the line of walkers and grabbed him in a bear hug. He looked startled. Annabelle started weeping.

Corentin turned his blue-tinted face up toward hers. His expression was pure confusion.

"Annabelle?" he said haltingly. He was dusty and looked tired.

She had never cried like this in her life. She couldn't speak. The tears gushed out of her eyes like water from a faucet. A tear fell from her face onto the shoulder of Corentin's brown fisherman's jacket. A little puff of dust exploded off the oil-treated fabric as the drop hit it.

Annabelle stood, holding her brother. The tears streaming out of her eyes dropped onto his upturned face like rain. As each drop touched his face, there was a little splash and the blue tint of the skin around where the drop hit got a little lighter.

"Annabelle?" Corentin said again, a little more firmly this time. He frowned like he was trying to solve a puzzle.

"Why are you here?" he said. He stopped and looked around himself. "Where are we?"

Annabelle glanced up as Llyr and Hades walked toward them. "Corentin," she said hurriedly, "I love you. I came to get you. I'm taking you home."

69

Llyr and Hades approached Annabelle and Corentin. Llyr hardly spared a glance for Corentin, as if he were invisible. Hades looked at him with curiosity. It seemed like he noticed the marks of Annabelle's tears on Corentin's face.

"We've had a little talk," said Llyr. "Let's try this again, shall we?"

Hades looked at Annabelle with an expressionless face. He might as well have been watching to see which branch of a stream a stick would float down.

"This is my brother, Corentin," Annabelle said.

"Ah, yes, the landlubber," said Llyr.

Annabelle looked at him from under a brow so furrowed, it seemed like a plow might have gotten stuck. If Llyr was a smarter man or god, he would have seen that look and been very careful about what he said next.

"It's a bit of a coincidence, that among all the people down here, you should happen to run into your brother," Llyr said. He frowned slightly and looked over at Hades.

Hades shrugged, his face still expressionless.

Annabelle pressed on her leg to stop it from shaking and attempted her awkward curtsy again.

"My lord," she bowed her head toward Hades, "it was delightful to have met you." She turned to Llyr, "Perhaps it's time for us to take our leave, Lord Llyr."

"Annabelle," Llyr said. He looked a little confused. "You said you needed to meet my brother."

"And, met we have," said Annabelle. She bowed in Hades's

direction again. "A pleasure."

Llyr looked even more confused. Annabelle backed away a step. She pulled Corentin by the arm.

Hades stood a little taller, and his expression darkened. "I hope you don't think he's going with you," he said.

Annabelle's lower lip quivered. "He is," she said.

Llyr's confused face seemed to clear a little, like a cloud moving across the sky. The cloud darkened as his mood shifted from bewilderment toward anger.

"Why are you here, Annabelle?" he said.

70

Looking at his face, it was hard to see the anger building in Hades. It was more visible in the small changes in his stance and body position. He leaned forward, the fist that wasn't holding his bident scepter clenched, and his whole body tensed.

"He is one of mine," he said firmly, dispassionately. "I do not release my charges so easily."

Corentin, like a dog that knows his owners are talking about him, cowered behind Annabelle. Annabelle worried about him. Unlike the Duke, his time in the underworld seemed to have drained his strength and wit. She hoped a return to the world above would bring it back to him.

Hecate, who had followed Llyr and Hades, was watching the exchange with interest. She tapped Hades on the shoulder to get his attention. The barely suppressed anger in the way he turned in response to her tap would have left Annabelle catatonic.

Hecate was hardly fazed. She was a tall woman, dressed in a flowing dark red robe. She had a silver belt around her waist with a key ring attached to it, like Hades. She pulled Hades to one side and started talking urgently to him in a lowered tone of voice.

Llyr turned to Annabelle. Corentin stood behind her, holding on to her tunic with both hands.

"This was not the way this was supposed to go," he said sadly. "What happened to meeting my family to get to know me better?"

Annabelle cast her gaze down to the ground.

"I think I know you pretty well," she said.

Hades and Hecate were having a discussion. Annabelle could see them looking at her and Corentin.

Llyr looked hurt. "You don't know me at all," he said. "You don't know what you are giving up."

"You can't give up something you never had," said Annabelle.

Hades returned from his discussion with Hecate. He seemed less angry, or perhaps he had just gotten better at hiding it.

"You can give up a promise. You can give up a dream. You can give up a life that any mortal would dream of." Llyr started getting excited again, though the excitement and fervor were mixed with anger this time.

"You can give up a love that would have eclipsed the seven seas. You can give up a life with a god."

As he spoke, the ground trembled. Annabelle had trouble keeping her feet.

Llyr paused, his breathing a little ragged. He looked at Annabelle, sadly again, and said, "You had this planned from the beginning, didn't you? Clever girl."

"Not quite the beginning," said Annabelle.

71

Hades, his rage dissipated, was watching the discussion with interest. Llyr seemed to cycle from anger to sadness to something resembling admiration for Annabelle's nerve with each moment.

"And what makes you think you have any chance to leave here without my help, with or without your brother?" said Llyr. "My brother will not let you go, and if you forfeit my goodwill, you, a mortal, will be stranded in Hades without any protection."

"My lord," said Annabelle. Her voice shook but continued without pause. "You have made me a promise."

Hades was leaning forward, listening intently. There might have been a hint of a smile around the corners of his mouth.

Annabelle continued, "My understanding is that a promise is a thing of importance to your kind."

Llyr looked stunned. The cycle of emotions broke. The anger rose to the fore.

"You ..." he cried, "you do not play games with the gods! No one bests Poseidon!"

Llyr straightened, his face flushing with anger. The ground under Annabelle's feet started shaking. As Llyr straightened, he seemed to grow. He was already taller than most around him, but as he spoke, they shrank, or he got taller.

Breaker, standing behind them, reared up onto his back legs, pawed the air furiously with his forehooves, and neighed loudly enough to wake the dead.

Annabelle crouched down, pulled Corentin to her, and tried to shield him with her body.

Llyr grew, and as he grew, he changed. From somewhere, a massive silvery trident appeared. He held it lightly in his right hand, poised as if to throw. He was taller now, taller than anyone had a right to be. His hair shifted from the black with a silver lock to a full head of shimmering gray. His face aged, as well. Annabelle recognized the aspect of Poseidon from the statue in Ardstead. His eyes were still the blue-green of the sea, but they looked old, sad, and tired beneath the anger.

Hades continued to watch, he seemed content to let things play out.

The passing dead halted. Perhaps Breaker's call had woken them. Maybe even they weren't so far gone as to not be interested in the tableau. They stood in a crowd on the roadway, staring at the god manifesting in front of them.

The crowd wasn't wholly motionless, however. A man was pushing his way through the throng. Small polite interjections of "Sorry" and "Pardon me" could be heard.

Llyr was still growing. There was a flicker or flutter in the air, and for a moment, Annabelle saw an immense sea creature standing there. Tentacled, scaled, dripping with saltwater and seaweed. Then it was Poseidon's older aspect again, the trident still poised.

Why doesn't he throw it already, she thought, her body shaking, *just get it over with.*

The person pushing his way through the crowd stepped in between Llyr and Annabelle. He faced Llyr. It was Koalemos.

72

Cole looked the same as he had when he visited Annabelle in Chelle. Big, hard to ignore, but in an unassuming sort of way. He was, of course, dwarfed by Llyr's current aspect. Looming over Cole, the giant with the trident hesitated, his access to his target restricted. Some of the tension and, with it, some of the size seemed to leak out of his body. Cole nodded to Hades, still standing impassively off to one side.

"Koalemos," said Llyr, his body continuing to diminish, the black color starting to leech back into his hair, "Why are you here?"

"Why," said Cole with a smile and a light laugh, "I live here, Posey." He gestured over past the vast persimmon orchard. "Tartarus is just over there."

Annabelle looked up, her body still trembling and whispered, "Thank you, Cole."

"Also," continued Cole, "I owed someone a debt."

Llyr was now back to his familiar self. Cole's arrival seemed to have taken the wind out of his sails and disarmed his anger.

"I heard something about a promise, Posey," said Cole.

Llyr looked at Cole and shook his head. "Don't call me that," he said plaintively.

Annabelle stood and helped Corentin to his feet. She brushed some dust off his clothing.

"I should just leave you here for a thousand years," said Llyr resentfully to Annabelle. "That would teach you to disrespect the gods."

Annabelle looked directly at Llyr. She spoke quietly and carefully. "You didn't promise that I would return to the surface. You promised that you wouldn't leave me here. 'by all the stars in the sea, I promise I won't leave you in Hades.' If I stay here, you have to stay, as well."

Llyr looked at her. He seemed to be trying to understand what that would mean.

Hades broke his silence. He was carefully following the conversation.

"Well," he said, "we can't have anyone staying down here a thousand years that isn't supposed to be here, can we." For some reason, he looked nervous at the prospect.

"I have been told by the keeper of the keys that unlock the gates of death," Hades nodded at Hecate, "that this one," a further nod at Corentin, "is not done with the surface world yet."

He continued. "I have no claim on you," looking at Annabelle, "though I don't like seeing the living down here. So as not to inconvenience my brother, I renounce any and all claims on the young man, Corentin Fisher.

"This has been fun, young lady," he said with a lessening of the grimness of the line of his mouth, "I do enjoy seeing the great Poseidon discomfited."

Hades gestured to the members of his retinue and turned to walk back to his chariot.

Llyr was left standing awkwardly with Annabelle and Cole. He looked deflated.

"You're not going to make me walk you home?" said Llyr sadly to Annabelle.

Cole stepped forward, offering his arm to Annabelle and said, "If I might have the pleasure?"

Llyr snapped his fingers, Breaker ran forward, and in one smooth move, he was mounted. From the horse's back, he turned to Annabelle and said, "It's not everyone who can say they've bested a god. A tip of my cousin's imaginary hat to you, Annabelle Agatha Fisher." He reached up to his head, grabbed the imaginary hat, and swept it broadly through the air with a bow from the waist.

"Oh, before I forget," said Llyr. He produced a coin from somewhere and flipped it through the air to Annabelle.

Llyr and Breaker wheeled away and were soon lost beyond the crowd.

73

Annabelle, Corentin, and Cole walked up the trail that led through the hills. Llyr's "shortcut." Cole was in a blisteringly rosy good mood, Annabelle felt tired, and Corentin was dragging behind. Annabelle had to hold back periodically to tug on him to make sure he didn't stop.

"Isn't it a beautiful nebulously, indeterminate time of day, young lady?" Cole asked, with infuriating cheer. Annabelle looked around. The view of the valley below was pleasant in its own way. The hills on either side were smoothly covered with an unvarying layer of the blue-gray turf. You could see the road in the distance beneath them. The heavens overhead were an unending uniform gray expanse.

"If there were trees," said Cole, "and there were birds, I'm sure the birds would be singing in the trees."

"Lord Koalemos," said Annabelle, "I really appreciate your escort." Cole looked bothered at the use of his full name. Annabelle continued, "But, I'm tired. Could we rest for a moment?"

They stopped at what might have been the same spot where she, Breaker, and Llyr had rested previously. The flowing stream tinkled pleasantly. Corentin moved toward it as if to drink, but Annabelle stopped him.

As she touched his hand, he turned to her.

"Annabelle?" he said. It was the first thing he'd said since Llyr had left them. Annabelle smiled at him and nodded encouragingly. His face was still splotched with the blue-gray color that discolored the faces of the residents of Hades, but it looked like it might be showing some signs of recovery.

"Annabelle?" Corentin repeated, "I didn't think I'd see you again. At least not so soon. When did you die?"

74

The trail rejoined the main road. There were far fewer of the dead walking along the way here. Annabelle recognized the canyon that contained Cerberus's cave along the roadway ahead.

Corentin had come to a grudging acceptance of the idea that Annabelle wasn't dead. The idea that he might not be and that they were returning to the surface world was more than he could take. Annabelle was encouraged, though. With each step, he seemed to show a little more life.

Cole led them on, with unrelenting vigor. He seemed to be enjoying the outing.

"Cerberus has her cave just through those hills," he said. "Hopefully, she's asleep. If so, we should just let her be."

As they approached the cave, Annabelle anticipated the meeting. She didn't expect Cerberus to be asleep. She seemed to be very dedicated to her watchdog duties.

Sure enough, the fuzzy, three-headed avalanche of dog launched itself out of the cave as they tried to pass.

Annabelle was intimidated, even knowing what was coming. She could see how Cerberus would be an effective barrier to stop any of the dead from trying to leave Hades.

The barking, snarling, growling creature softened immediately as soon as she saw who was passing. Two heads started licking Annabelle's face, while the third pushed up against her hand. Cole got some attention too. Cerberus clearly knew and liked him. Corentin got himself some suspicious sideways looks.

As she had with Llyr before, Cerberus led Annabelle back into the cave to show off her puppies.

While she leaned over the edge of the nest, Annabelle began a soothing chatter for Cerberus.

"Oh, look how cute they are. Have they grown already since we saw them?"

Corentin was beside Annabelle, looking over the edge of the nest as well.

There was a rustling, swishing sort of sound, and Corentin slid down the side of the nest into the pile of writhing dogs.

"Corentin!" cried Annabelle. She had been looking at the puppies and hadn't seen if he had slipped and fallen or jumped.

Corentin disappeared into the mass of dog flesh. Nine heads, three bodies, and uncountable legs and little puppy paws. Some heads growled, some whined. Some nipped, some licked.

After a moment, Corentin reappeared, his head showing just above the jumble of puppy parts. He turned toward Annabelle, his face still splotched with the blue-gray pallor of the underworld. He turned toward Annabelle, his face splashed with puppy drool. He turned toward Annabelle, smiled at her, and laughed.

75

As they continued along the road that led from Cerberus's canyon to the river Styx, Annabelle looked at Corentin's face. The blotchiness seemed much better. Who knew that the cure for the pallor of death was puppy drool?

Corentin noticed Annabelle looking at him. He seemed to be regaining his awareness of what was going on around him.

"Annabelle," he said, "how are Mama and Papa?" He frowned and looked thoughtful for a moment. "I used to worry about them."

Annabelle felt her eyes welling with tears.

"They're good, Corentin," she said. "They will be so happy to see you."

The low cloud of fog that cloaked the riverbank came into view as they neared the river. There was a sharp line where the fog began. Moving into the fog bank, Annabelle shivered with the chill.

When they reached the dock and the river, there was no ferryboat in sight.

Stepping onto the boards, Cole said, "We might have a bit of a wait. The ferry doesn't run from this side."

There wasn't anything like a bench, just the unadorned dock. The other side had at least had the boathouse. Cole saw Annabelle looking and said, "The dead do not need to rest, and the living don't come here often."

Charon's punt came gliding through the fog toward the

dock. Annabelle had no idea how long they had been waiting. Between the silence, the gray of the fog, and the mood of the underworld, she had lost all ability to estimate time.

The punt bumped up against the dock. Cole stepped forward and grabbed the dock line. Charon, standing in the back of the boat, just looked coldly at him.

When the punt pulled up alongside the dock, the passengers unloaded. Annabelle had become somewhat familiar with the presence of the dead while traveling through the underworld. Still, there was something different about standing here as these newcomers stepped off the boat for the first time.

They showed more emotion than the dead the travelers had seen on the roads. Some of these people were grieving, some seemed angry. They flowed by Corentin, Annabelle, and Cole like water flowing past rocks. Though new to the underworld, they all seemed to know where they were going. They headed down the road toward the Halls of Judgment.

There were too many for the size of the punt. Many, too many. Annabelle lost count of how many people moved past her as she stood there.

She lost count, and then she stopped trying to count. One of the dead, stepping off the boat trying to pass her, was her father.

76

Annabelle dropped to her knees in front of him, blocking his path. She could feel her eyes filling with tears again. "Papa," she cried. Corentin stood stock-still behind her. Cole stayed a few steps back.

Mr. Fisher stopped, standing in front of her. The pallor of the underworld had not yet fully set into his features.

"Annabelle?" he said slowly. The anger and grief on the faces of some of the dead did not show on his face. He seemed calmer.

"And Corentin," he continued, "I hoped that I would see you both again." He held out his arms. "Come and give your papa a hug."

Annabelle stood. Corentin rushed into his father's arms. It didn't seem that their father knew, or understood, which direction they were going.

Annabelle sobbed, "Papa, it's all my fault. I drank some water, and Llyr said that someone would die. I never thought it would be you."

"Of course, it's not your fault, Annabelle," Mr. Fisher said, "It was my time. My day was done."

"But Papa, I just saw you yesterday," said Annabelle.

"Did you?" said Mr. Fisher.

"Come with us, Papa," said Annabelle. "I'm taking Corentin out. You can come too."

"Out?" said Mr. Fisher. "I can't do that, Annabelle. They're waiting for me." He waved in the direction the other dead had gone. "Fisher men are fishermen."

Charon, who was watching the conversation from the back of his punt, said, "We had an enjoyable conversation about fishing on the boat ride over. Your father is very knowledgeable." Then he muttered, shook his head, and tried to act like he hadn't said anything.

"Give us a hug, Annabelle," said Mr. Fisher. He was still holding Corentin, but he opened up his arms wider and gestured her in.

Annabelle joined in the hug with her brother. She squeezed up against her father's chest. He was colder than she remembered, but the slight smell of the fishing boat that never left him made her feel like she was home.

"I'm just happy my babies will see the sun again," said Mr. Fisher.

77

Cole was trying to negotiate a fare with Charon. Charon was having none of it and almost seemed to refuse to accept the concept. "It doesn't work that way," he said. "I ferry people into the underworld, not out."

"I have taken it upon myself to help this young lady and her brother," said Cole. "I will not be stymied by a small-minded bureaucrat."

For a moment, Annabelle was convinced that the end of Charon's pole would meet the back of Cole's head. She decided it was time to intercede.

"Charon," she said, "you can tell we're alive. We're not supposed to be here." Corentin had lost almost all of the unearthly pallor of the underworld.

Charon looked thoughtful. "I'm not even sure what the fare should be," he said slowly.

"Do you need to charge us a fare?" said Annabelle.

Charon just looked at her. The expression on his face made it clear that he thought the question made her stupider than she thought Caspian Fisher.

Cole weighed in again. "You have let people through from this side before. Hercules, Orpheus, Theseus. What fare did they pay?"

"Orpheus sang me a song," said Charon. "It was very pretty. Butterflies and flowers." A teardrop formed below his fierce eye at the memory. It looked out of place on his grizzled, surly old face.

His expression changed. "Hercules took my pole away

from me and hit me with it. Then, he poled across himself. Theseus, of course, was with him. I had to swim across to get back to my boat." His expression showed that the experience still rankled him.

Annabelle thought she saw her way. "Charon," she said as kindly as she could. "You enjoyed your conversation with my father, didn't you? You heard him say that he wanted to have his children see the sun again? He was a customer of yours, could you let us pass for him?"

78

They passed through the archway at the entrance to Hades and started up the flagstone tunnel that she and Llyr had come down an eternity ago. Annabelle tried to engage her brother in conversation. He kept looking around at their surroundings like a newborn seeing the world for the first time.

The tunnel was warm and narrow. Since they'd left the ambient gray glow of the underworld, their only light source was a glowing red stone that Cole had pulled out of a pocket when they first entered the dark tunnel. The light was ominously blood-like, but it was bright enough to see by. Cole told Annabelle that Hecate had given it to him.

As they reached a point in the tunnel where they could see a glimmer of what looked like daylight ahead, Cole stopped.

"My dear," he said, "it has been my great pleasure traveling with you." He reached out and rumpled the hair on Corentin's head. "And you, too, of course.

"I'm afraid I have to leave you," he continued. "Up ahead is an exit from the underworld. Be proud, both of you, for you are the first living people to leave Hades in a thousand years."

Annabelle moved over to Cole, leaned forward, and kissed him on the cheek.

"Thanks for everything," she said.

As Cole faded, the red glow of the stone he was holding faded with him. The tunnel dimmed into almost total darkness. The only light was the glimmer of daylight from the tunnel mouth in the distance. Annabelle reached out and felt around in the dark for her brother's hand.

They walked together through the tunnel mouth and out into the bright light of the morning sun.

79

As they stepped out of the tunnel onto the Western Way, Annabelle looked at Corentin. The last traces of the blotchiness from the underworld were washed away by the morning sun. Corentin looked back at her.

"Annabelle?" he said. "Are we really here?"

Annabelle looked around. They stood in the alcove off the Western Way, where her underworld adventure with Llyr had begun. The tunnel mouth that they had just stepped through was gone. There was a solid rock wall behind them. The sun shone overhead, but she could see the Chelle clouds waiting to cover it and bring back the familiar gray cloudy skies. The sea glimmered in the reflected sunlight just to their north, and sea birds were making their raucous calls overhead. The smell of salt was in the air.

"Yes, Corentin," she said, "We're really here."

There was what looked like a campsite set up in the alcove. A small tent, a pile of firewood, a rough bench made of piled stones, and a fire pit were neatly laid out. Annabelle walked over to the pit. The embers were still warm from a campfire from the night before. She glanced in the tent. There was no one inside.

Corentin stood, looking at the seabirds, the cloudy skies, and the sea. He took a deep breath, filling his lungs with the salty air.

She walked over to him and took his hand again.

"Corentin, let's go home."

80

As Annabelle and Corentin walked down the Western Way toward home, the realization that her father wouldn't be there when she opened the door to their cottage set in. She felt her eyes start to water. Annabelle shook her head angrily. She could grieve for her father, but she was tired of crying.

She looked over at Corentin. The expression of confusion on his face had been replaced by excitement. Of course, for him, his whole family and the entire world had been lost forever. It was probably hard to think about what it meant to have seen their father at the ferry when he was about to regain so much.

She started to get excited, as well. Even though it had only been a few days, she felt like it was forever since she had seen Bellarose and her mother.

"Corentin," she said, "you know that it's been a long time since you..." she found it hard to say "died."

Corentin turned to her, his face shining with excitement. The last trace of the pallor from the underworld was gone. He looked like a handsome, healthy youth. She felt a flush of pride at what she had done for him.

"I know, Annabelle," he said, "about how long do you think it was?"

Annabelle looked at him and thought about it for a moment. "I guess you're about as much younger than me than I was younger than you before," she concluded hesitantly.

"So, you're the older sister now," said Corentin with a laugh. The life flooding back into him seemed to be bubbling over. It was infectious.

"I'm gonna see Soggy," said Corentin, "And Bella!" He looked at Annabelle. "Is she still a little brat?" he said.

Annabelle didn't have time to answer.

"And Mama!" he continued. "And Pa ...," he slowed down and stopped. "I guess not Papa," he said sadly.

"Corentin," said Annabelle, "he got to see you again. I'm sure that made him very happy."

They reached the path that led from the Way to their little courtyard and started down it.

81

Annabelle opened the door to their little cottage. She stepped inside and called out eagerly, "Bella, Bella, I'm home, I'm home!" Corentin was right on her heels. She looked at him, corrected herself, and called out, "We're home!"

Annabelle looked around the room. There were more changes than she expected. It felt less lived in, somehow. It was mostly just a lack of clutter. Her mother must have just straightened up.

Annabelle heard her mother's voice, familiar and reassuring, calling out from the other room.

"Who's there? Bellarose doesn't live here anymore."

Mrs. Fisher walked into the room, saw Annabelle and Corentin standing near the doorway, and stopped dead. Her jaw dropped open.

"Oh, my," she said.

Mrs. Fisher looked tired and sad, but mostly, at the moment, she looked shocked.

Annabelle rushed to explain.

"Mama, it's just me. I brought Corentin back with me."

"Oh, my," said Mrs. Fisher.

"What did you mean that Bellarose doesn't live here anymore? I brought Corentin back from the land of the dead. It's all right, he's not dead anymore."

Mrs. Fisher shook her head. Trying to clear out some cobwebs, or perhaps trying to stir in some baffling information.

"But, Annabelle," she said, "You're dead too."

82

Annabelle frowned. "Of course, I'm not dead, Mama," she said. "I just left a few days ago to find Corentin. Llyr was Poseidon. We went to the underworld. I met the gods there. Cerberus has puppies!"

Mrs. Fisher's mouth got stern. It firmed up into a single straight line when she set her children, or her husband, straight.

"Annabelle, you've been dead for three years. I should know. I mourned you."

Annabelle felt like a naughty child. For a moment, she felt like stamping her foot.

"I'm here, Mama, and this is Corentin."

The sternness faded from Mrs. Fisher's face. She started crying.

"Corentin," she said, "and Annabelle ..." She slumped to her knees. Corentin and Annabelle rushed over to her and held her.

Mrs. Fisher was recovering on a bench. Corentin and Annabelle tried to calm her.

"Your father is dead," she said sadly.

"We know," said Annabelle.

"He would have been so happy to see you two," she paused. "I must be dead, as well."

"You're not dead, Mama," said Annabelle, "and neither are we."

"This doesn't happen," said Mrs. Fisher. The stern mouth seemed about to make an appearance again.

"It did, Mama," said Annabelle. "What did you mean

about Bellarose not living here anymore?"

"Corentin. My baby." Mrs. Fisher reached out and drew the boy to her. "You look exactly like you did on that day."

"Mkrhtsd ..." said Corentin from where his head was buried in his mother's chest.

"Bella doesn't live here anymore; I live alone now. Although, I've been thinking about moving in with Bella and her husband, to help with the little one," said Mrs. Fisher.

Annabelle just looked at her in stunned silence.

"They named her Annabelle."

83

Annabelle looked around with fresh eyes. *Was it possible that it really had been three years since she left?* She looked again at her mother. As the reality of Annabelle and Corentin being there set in, some of her sadness was fading. But even with her happier expression, she looked older. Her hair had gone from salt and pepper to full gray. She seemed to carry herself less upright as if the years had worn on her.

"Bellarose got married?" Annabelle exclaimed.

"Of course, she did," said Mrs. Fisher. "Ewan is a nice boy."

"Ewan Bellwether?"

"Of course," said Mrs. Fisher. "There aren't any other Ewans in town."

"I'll have to talk to her about that," said Annabelle. *Bellarose Bellwether?* She thought.

Annabelle looked around at the inside of the cottage. It wasn't that her mother had straightened up, the room had changed. It looked lived in, in a different way. Anything that showed that Annabelle or Bellarose had lived there was gone, and there were other changes. Her eye was drawn to some things on the mantelpiece below the fragment from Caspian's vinscif.

The things stood out in their simple home: a velvet-lined, glass-covered case containing what looked like some kind of medal, and a gilt frame around a portrait of her father.

"Mama," said Annabelle, "what are those?" She pointed at the mantelpiece.

Mrs. Fisher turned to see what Annabelle was pointing at. She loosened her grip on Corentin. He pulled away, gasping for breath.

"Your father," she said, pride filling her voice, "died a hero."

Annabelle walked over to the mantle and looked at the case. It was gilded wood, a glass door, and a red velvet bed holding what looked like a gold medal. The medal had the ducal seal, her father's name, and the engraved words "Our eternal gratitude."

"About six months after you disappeared," said Mrs. Fisher, "your father was fishing, and an unexpected storm came up. The duke's cog was out sailing, and it floundered. Your father came to the rescue. He saved the duke's life!"

84

Annabelle looked at her mother. She glowed with pride. It seemed that her husband's heroism was something she had held on to as a source of strength since he died. Annabelle tried to imagine what her mother had been through.

"Mama," she said, "I think the duke's dead."

Mrs. Fisher nodded apologetically. "Of course, you're right, Annabelle. I meant the new duke. The old duke drowned when the ship went down. It was his nephew, Finley, who held on to a spar long enough for your father to get there. He's the duke now.

"We went to the castle, Annabelle. The new duke gave a speech. He's such a nice young man. He told everyone how your father saved his life. He said such sweet things about your father, about Chelle, and about the Fishers."

"But, Mama," said Annabelle, "what happened after that? How did he die?"

Mrs. Fisher looked sad again. The conversation really seemed to be bringing her through highs and lows.

"It's not your fault, Annabelle, but it was you and Corentin. It was about six months later. His heart was weak, and he never got over you and Corentin. A parent shouldn't have to outlive their children."

"How have you been managing alone?" said Annabelle.

"Bella and Ewan have been helping," said Mrs. Fisher. "But the money's running out. Your father and I never had a lot. That's part of why I've been thinking about moving in with them."

Annabelle pulled her shoulder bag off. She looked inside for her coin purse.

"Mama," she said, "I don't have much, but I have the money I took with me when I left." She dumped the contents of the purse out on the table. One coin fell to the tabletop with a resounding thud. It was the coin Llyr had tossed to her when he left. She had stuffed it into the purse without looking at it. It was solid gold.

85

Mrs. Fisher had gone to tell the wives' circle about the miracle, as she called it. If you wanted some information spread around Chelle by the Sea as quickly as possible, there was no better way than to tell it to the wives' circle.

Annabelle and Corentin stayed home. They weren't ready to face any of the townspeople yet.

The door swung open, and Bellarose came inside. She had a fabric baby sling tied around one shoulder. Little Annabelle's blond curls peeked out from the top.

She came inside, saw Annabelle sitting on a bench by the dining table, and stopped.

"I thought she was raving," she said quietly. "I thought she'd finally lost it."

Annabelle leapt to her feet. "Bella!" she called out.

Bellarose backed up, partway out the door, and lifted her hands, palms outward, in front of her. She mumbled something under her breath.

"Bella," said Annabelle sadly.

"Annabelle?" said Bellarose. "Is it really you?" She stepped back inside the doorframe, clutching the baby in the sling tightly enough that she started to fuss.

"It's me, Bella," said Annabelle, she started moving forward again. More than anything, she wanted to give her sister a hug.

Bellarose started crying. "I want to believe it's you, Annabelle, but it doesn't make any sense."

Annabelle grabbed her into a hug. She squeezed so hard

that the baby's fuss turned into a cry.

Corentin poked his head through the doorframe. He had been in the other room.

"Hi, Bella," he said.

Bellarose looked at him and started crying harder. The baby heard her and began screaming. If Annabelle hadn't known better, she might have made a comment about waking Poseidon's brother.

86

Bellarose, Corentin, and Annabelle sat at the dining room table. Bella looked at Annabelle, her bright blue eyes opened wide, and said, "Anna, how is this possible? Things like this just don't happen."

Annabelle looked at the floor for a moment, then looked up and met her sister's gaze. "How is it possible that you caught Ewan Bellwether?" said Annabelle, "He was the one all the girls tried to get."

Bellarose looked at her feet and blushed prettily. Annabelle looked at the sweet pink flush on her sister's cheek, the curl of blond hair partly covering it, and thought, *that's how it's possible.*

Corentin seemed to have recovered his youthful energy. He looked at Annabelle. "Anna," he said, "how long do we have to wait before we can go to town? I want to see what some of my friends are doing."

Little Annabelle was crawling around on the floor. Bellarose had put down a blanket for her. She hadn't started walking yet, but she moved well enough to get into trouble. She grabbed at Annabelle's dress.

Annabelle picked up her niece. In what felt like a few days, her family had changed so dramatically, it was unrecognizable.

Annabelle started to bounce the baby on her knee.

"I was thinking," she said, "that we should let the news of our return travel around the town for a little. Otherwise, we'll have to explain ourselves to everyone over and over again."

Bellarose had a thought. She laughed. "You know," she said, "I'm the older sister now. If Corentin is the age he was when he …," like Annabelle had had previously, she had trouble saying the word, "left. And, you're the same age as you were when you … left, then I'm older than both of you."

She stood up and moved over next to Corentin. She tried her best to tower over him. "Who's the annoying little brat now," she said. Corentin stood up. The towering effect was spoiled by the fact that they were almost exactly the same height.

87

Bellarose told the story of their father's adventure with the new duke. "He was so proud, Anna. He told me how, when he first pulled the new duke (though, he wasn't the duke then, he was just the duke's nephew)... when he first pulled him out of the water, he just lay in the bottom of the boat, and looked like a drowned rat."

"It's hard to imagine Finley looking like that," said Annabelle.

Bellarose looked shocked. "He's the duke, Anna. You shouldn't be so familiar."

She continued, "Anyway, he looked like a drowned rat, and Papa was still sailing around looking for other survivors. After a while, the new duke asked Papa what his name was. When he said Fisher, the duke asked him if he had any daughters. Papa told him he had two."

Bellarose nodded along with her own story. "We all got to meet him. There was a big to-do at his castle. You should have heard the nice things he said about Papa. He gave him a medal."

Bellarose pointed to the mantelpiece. Annabelle nodded acknowledgment.

"He's changed things, Anna," said Bellarose. "He set up a committee to work on making things better between Chelle and Ardstead. He said, 'If the fishermen of Chelle can save his life, he can improve the lives of the fishermen of Chelle.'"

Bellarose drew in a deep breath. "He's so nice, Anna. Ewan is on the committee. He says that they really listen, sometimes."

Corentin lay on the floor, playing with little Annabelle. "Isn't it going to be confusing, having two Annabelles?" he said.

Bellarose frowned. "That wasn't going to be a problem." She looked accusatively at her sister.

88

A few days later, Annabelle walked along the Western Way toward town. She was nervous but felt that it was time. Her mother said that their return was the only thing that anyone in Chelle talked about, and people were curious to see them. She had been holding them off, saying that Annabelle and Corentin needed to rest, but the pressure was building.

It was a nice morning, for Chelle. The sun fought its way through the clouds enough that it wasn't cold. Or at least not as cold as it could have been. The air was full of the smell of the sea, and the seabirds flew overhead, taking off and landing on perches on the cliffs. The sound of their cries was comforting to Annabelle.

Corentin would come with her tomorrow. They had decided that they should reintroduce themselves to the townsfolk, gradually, and Corentin's return was even more shocking than Annabelle's. She had, after all, been a disappearance. People knew Corentin had drowned.

There was a young man walking toward Annabelle. He looked like he might be about her age, or perhaps a year or two older. She looked at him curiously as he approached. He was tall, broad-shouldered, and handsome. He had the blue-green eyes of the sea and a head of thick brown hair. She had been used to immediately ignoring anyone with those eyes, but somehow they didn't bother her anymore.

He wore clothes that weren't out-of-place in Chelle, so

she was confident he was a local. She felt sure she should recognize him, and as they got closer together, she did.

"Jonah?" she said.

"Annabelle," Jonah said, calmly, almost serenely.

89

Jonah smiled at her. The boy she had known was in that smile, but there was something else there as well. A maturity that hadn't been there before, or perhaps it was just that he had grown into a tall, handsome young man. Annabelle felt her heart beat a little faster.

"Annabelle," he repeated, "I've heard the stories they're telling in town. You look exactly the same as on the day you left."

Annabelle felt like she should be moving forward to hug him, but it didn't seem to be what he was expecting. She wondered when his shoulders had gotten so broad. He must have been working with his father on the fishing boat for the last few years. She remembered him saying that he was going to.

"Annabelle?" said Jonah. He smiled at her again.

It was the tan, too, the fisherman's tan. He wasn't keeping himself as covered up as he should on the fishing boat. Fisherfolk needed to protect themselves from the sun and the salt spray.

"Did you leave your tongue behind in the underworld?" he asked. "Do you remember how I used to tell people I was going to marry you?"

She did remember. She remembered complaining to Bellarose that it was annoying. It didn't feel as annoying anymore.

"I really meant it," said Jonah. "I was sure it was going to happen. I guess I shouldn't have married Cordelia Cuttlecutter."

Annabelle took a step back. Her heart sank in her chest.

"Cordelia Cuttlecutter," she said, "congratulations."

Jonah saw her reaction. He took a step forward to match her step back.

"I'm kidding, Anna," he said. "I wouldn't marry anyone but you. I saw you and that Llyr leave. I saw you walk through the cliff face. I waited for you. I knew you were coming back to me. I watched for you."

Annabelle blinked tears from her eyes. She stepped forward.

Jonah pulled her into the hug she had been looking for from the beginning.

Annabelle felt like she was home.

EPILOGUE

With new support from the duke, Chelle by the Sea became a prosperous town. The sea favored the town more than other towns along the coast, and the fishing was good.

Corentin joined the duke's guard when he came of age. He wanted to serve, and Finley remembered his family's service and that the sea was not for him. He became trusted enough that he was assigned to guard King Twilight's room when the king visited the coast.

Annabelle, the elder, and Jonah were married. Bellarose cried at the wedding.

Annabelle, the younger, grew into a beautiful young woman. Her beauty developed a reputation. It was said by some that her face made the angels cry, and her eyes put the sea waves to shame.

But those are tales for another time.

BY THE SEA

Dear Reader,

I hope you've enjoyed *By the Sea*. The adventures are just beginning, so if you'd like to join another one, please email lampreypublishing-@gmail.com with your contact email address. You'll receive exclusive email notifications as new books in this world are released.

 I also hope you'll consider dropping a quick review at the store where you bought this book,

Thank you for reading!

ACKNOWLEDGEMENT

Thanks to my beta readers, Claudia, John, Page, and Nancy. Also, as always, to my alpha, Andrea.

And special thanks to Judy Thurlow for editing. Commas should be where they should, and quotation marks need to respect their boundaries.

BOOKS BY THIS AUTHOR

Moon & Shadow

Standing on the cow pasture fence, Sebastian pulls the moon down from the sky. This starts a chain of events that leads to battles with monsters, an epic journey, and a confrontation with a channeler of nightmares.

Unsure what's happening to him, Sebastian has to fight to save his small medieval village and the woman he loves from destruction.

With his fellow villager's support, Sebastian journeys to find the source of the creatures that embody the worst of our dreams.

Where are the nightmares coming from? Who is attacking a simple farming village, and why?

And, once he reaches and confronts the source, how will Sebastian, the Knight of Moon and Shadow, overcome it?

The Wolf's Tooth

A young boy walking along a shadowy path through a forest runs into a pack of wolves-just the first step on Twee's journey from boyhood to manhood in a magical kingdom.

A forest fire, a prison cell, an outlaw band, each time Twee turns his head, his life gets a little more out of control.

Enslaved and then forced to work as a blacksmith's apprentice, Twee meets Vix, a flame-haired street urchin who needs him as much as he needs her.

Why does the cruel Young Lion, the prince regent of the realm, drag Twee into his dungeons in chains? What connection is there between the young, powerless Twee and the most powerful man in the kingdom?

The Wolf's Tooth follows the misadventures of Twee as he grows from a boy to a man.

Made in the USA
Middletown, DE
19 October 2020